DARK MATTERS

QUICK READS FOR ADVENTUROUS MINDS

RICK BOBRICK

Published by Red Penguin Books

Bellerose Village, New York

ISBN

Digital 978-1-63777-767-1

Print 978-1-63777-787-9

Library of Congress Control Number: 2025917911

THE INNARDS

INTRODUCTION

Welcome reader! I sincerely hope that you will like this collection of short stories as much as I enjoyed writing them. I kept them short and sweet to accommodate hurried lives and wavering attention spans. Writing with brevity was more challenging than I imagined. It forced me to choose my words and phrases with extra care. So, do not be fooled into reading hastily; a slow and thoughtful approach will help you get the most out of each of these 27 quick reads.

Suspense, science fiction, horror, fantasy, and the supernatural predominate this collection. Many of these stories will take you on journeys to dark and even disturbing places. You will also find several hopeful and magical side trips scattered along the way. All in all, if these stories do their job, you will be left with an adventurous mind, well satisfied – and plenty of time to spare!

Rick Bobrick

Medusa, New York

Spring 2025

ACKNOWLEDGMENTS

First and foremost, I would like to thank my small group of reliable and helpful test readers. Denis, Frank, Diane, Jason, Homer, and my daughter Emily. Each and every one of them is smart, opinionated, well-read, and honest. Collectively they convinced me I had stories well worth reading. Thank you all for your time and your valuable feedback.

Rod Serling and Steven King deserve a nod of thanks for influencing much of what you will find in these pages. A belated thank you to Mr. Boyce for teaching us the power and beauty of words, and for trying to convince us to never use the word, "thing" (A point well taken and a 50-year-old lesson never forgotten).

And special thanks to my publicist, Stephanie Larkin and her assistant Denise Reichert at Red Penguin Books. Their support and encouragement was unwavering, especially after my decision to move from writing children's picture books to writing this collection of dark and somewhat disturbing short stories.

*Dedicated to all those readers with attention spans
that have been diminished by the lure of the internet.
You have my deepest empathy.*

1

THE VISITATION

We Come In Peace

It sat in a large field in upstate New York emitting a low frequency hum. The spacecraft was surrounded by an impenetrable force field that the NASA aerospace forensic team discovered the hard way. The proximity sensors on their mobile ground robot alarmed wildly, just before it vaporized in a blinding flash of white light.

"Damn Alan, that was one expensive sparkler. Our bot didn't get within ten meters of that thing. Now what?"

"I don't think we have too many options . . . unless you want to give it a try, Walt."

"Only if you take the lead, skipper."

Alan gave him *that* look and addressed his team, "I'm scrubbing the active investigation. Our only option left is patience."

And they didn't have to wait long.

The next day, a message appeared on every mobile device on Earth: "We come in Peace. You are to expect an operating system update on this device that will include our voice-to-text translation software.

The many dozens of your most common languages and dialects will be readily accommodated, as our communication here demonstrates. We will be exiting our vehicle tomorrow at 12:00 pm, EDT."

At the field in upstate New York, the spacecraft's low frequency humming stopped right on schedule and the occupants emerged from their ship. People around the world viewed the live stream with excitement, curiosity, and even a bit of apprehension. The aliens were human-like in appearance but with a bulbous braincase and imposing stature. Their spoken language was deep and garbled, as if they were speaking in tongues. Their opening statement gave a glimpse of their superior intellect, "You will be pleased to know that we have the ability to understand all Earth languages, both written and spoken. This will assure straightforward, two-way communications. The purpose of our visit will be provided when a proper setting can be arranged."

The low frequency hum returned as soon as they re-entered their spaceship.

The Visitation, as it came to be known, left many overwhelmed with humility. The internet exploded in a shockwave of hyper-virality . Governments froze as the world order was about to be shaken to its core. The very foundations of world religions lay in ruins as the gods we made were no longer relevant. Astrophysicists and exobiologists celebrated the arrival of their holy grail. Humans everywhere were on pins and needles as the reason for this otherworldly visit hung heavily in the air.

Help for Humanity

The alien crew was invited to speak at a UN General Assembly session in New York City. International leaders and experts of every stripe sat spellbound as the alien commander delivered his message. "Good evening humans. We hope that our sudden arrival did not alarm you. Our surveillance drones indicated that assistance would be most advantageous at this time. To facilitate precise communications, understand that we have complete knowledge of your nomenclature systems, as well as the many billions of your proper names.

Though our syntax and grammar may be imperfect, the technical language required to advance our mission will be flawless. Please know that we have come to your world in peace, offering a book of gifts that we call, *Helpings of Humanity*. As you examine each of these extraordinary gifts, suspicions will be understandable. In fact, it may all seem too good to be true. We vow to earn your trust and respect as we will work closely with your engineers and scientists, providing expertise at every turn of your journey. We most firmly do believe that alliances with our galactic neighbors are essential for a universe no longer constrained by the speed of light. Do not mistake us for generous or altruistic beings as those concepts have no meaning in our world. However, we do wish you great success as you will be joining a planetary coalition that wants nothing more than to serve you well."

This was followed by a question-and-answer session that had attendees and viewers alike staring in awe as translations of those deep and garbled voices filled their screens. The alien's pleasant yet serious demeanor and encouraging message helped to put people's minds at ease. Any left-over concerns were replaced by hope – and many felt a deep, almost a spiritual connection to these visitors from space.

Helpings of Humanity was offered in every major language in the developed world. It was a comprehensive, digital tome that presented alien technologies in stunning detail. Scientists, engineers, and medical experts were astonished by the vast array of advanced technical information that was bestowed by this mysterious race of extraterrestrials. Solutions to problems that might have taken hundreds of years of human brain evolution to solve were presented on a proverbial silver platter. For the more skeptical, it really did seem too good to be true.

The Gifts

The early chapters provided sophisticated manufacturing and construction techniques, exquisite engineering drawings, advanced AI software tools, and complex chemical formulas, equations, and reaction procedures. The most critical chapter described the large-scale synthesis of elements 121 and 123. These surprisingly stable synthetic metals and their alloys possessed properties that were essential for the production of many of the new technologies gifted to humanity.

One by one, each succeeding chapter revealed solutions for the most threatening problems facing the human race. Thermodynamic engineering systems for lowering global atmospheric and oceanic temperatures along with highly efficient CO_2 sequestration technologies. Carbon-free nuclear fusion reactors for generating electricity. Room temperature superconducting electrical transmission systems capable of transforming the world's power grid. Unfathomable medical cures for all known diseases and addictions. Gene splicing procedures to significantly increase human longevity. Agricultural advances that could feed an overpopulated planet while providing optimal dietary intake. And inter-stellar transportation systems for accessing the complex network of wormholes scattered across the universe.

One of the most promising technologies was intended to alleviate the overpopulation of our planet. More than 12 billion people were crowded into Earth's dwindling number of thermally habitable zones. World leaders agreed to take on the construction of hundreds of Molecular Transporter Centers for the relocation of humans. In order to entice people to leave the hellscape of late 21st century Earth the aliens provided video tours of their home planet and the Utopia that awaited.

A Home Away From Home

Their planet was located in a binary solar system located 5.72 million light years away in the Andromeda galaxy. It was gravity and climate-controlled with all the necessary accommodations in place for human arrivals. Stunning landscapes and vistas, a pale blue sky complete with dual sunrises and sunsets, and geographic features that were identical to Earth's most beautiful locations. Newly constructed towns and cities were filled with charming residences, parks, theatres, shops, walkways, and streets. Restaurants offered the most delicious assortment of familiar comfort foods along with every exotic, cultural cuisine on Earth. And best of all, there were no screens, no internet, or social media platforms to erode the attention span of humans or to distract them from the wonderment of their new world. Wealth, power, class, fear, hatred, and war were all concepts long forgotten in this home away from home.

Deep in the Heart of Seoul

A concerning discovery made by a team of South Korean computer scientists set off their personal alarm bells. It was the existence of a text that was secretly encrypted into *Helpings of Humanity*. It was written in an alien language so complex that even the most advanced AI tools were unable to translate it. However, the significance of their discovery gave them all the motivation they needed to persist. Using quantum computing systems and tens of thousands of hours of run-time, they were able to crack the alien code.

The four engineers huddled in a super-secure facility below the teeming nightlife of Seoul. The years of exhausting and tedious work had finally paid off. They remained hopeful as their decoded translation began to run. Their optimism quickly vanished as a nearly endless stream of short, three-page, illustrated chapters scrolled across their screens.

The team leader, Kim Soo-young was the first to break the shocked silence. "No! It can't be." she cried, "These are recipes. Dozens and dozens of recipes! Appetizers, entrees, side dishes, and desserts – and we're the main ingredient in every one of them."

IT specialist Lee Minho had a sudden flashback. "Helpings of humanity . . . Serve us well . . . Too good to be true . . . Christ Almighty, their real mission was hiding in plain sight."

Kim Soo-young and her colleagues sat speechless as their thoughts turned to the hundreds of Molecular Transporter Centers around the world and the millions of people who had already left our planet for theirs – only to wind up on alien menus.

Their stunned silence was ruptured by the metallic disconnect of electromagnetic deadbolts and the slow swing of the heavy door as it opened – followed by deep and garbled voices that needed no translation.

2

SUMMER BLITZ

Henry loved to eat fish almost as much as he loved catching them. In fact, he often caught and kept more than he and his family could eat. He paid close attention to the tide charts and weather forecasts; he followed the fishing reports religiously and took great pride in his gear preparation the night before each trip. It was all about being an efficient angler – a killing machine. When Henry woke up on this warm summer morning, he could not have possibly predicted how an insane blitz of feeding bluefish would end.

Bluefish are vicious predators – such voracious killers they become easy targets for anglers when they go on the type of feeding frenzy Henry encountered. As he walked the beach to his lucky spot at the end of the jetty a flock of gulls and terns hovered above a froth of churning whitewater as bluefish were slaughtering a bait ball of menhaden trapped at the surface. Henry picked up the pace knowing full well the action would be fast and furious.

And boy, was it ever. Within the first hour Henry caught seven blues all over 10 pounds from his lucky spot at the end of the jetty. Cast, after cast, after cast, after cast produced savage strikes from the school of ravenous feeders. He was as good a killing machine as his quarry. Because of their extremely aggressive behavior when landed

Henry took the usual precautions to prevent being bitten when unhooking each bluefish. He would step on their struggling bodies while taking care to avoid their gnashing , razor sharp teeth as multiple sharp blows to the head with his Billy club finished the job. Henry would then fling his fish onto the beach in a rush to make his next cast. The bloody rock where he killed his prey was a testament to his success on this warm summer morning.

As the action slowed down, Henry was surprised to see a sandwich lying on one of massive rocks that formed the man-made jetty. Though he didn't remember packing it, he assumed his wife had made it to surprise him. He was unhappy that it had fallen out of his gear bag but pleased that the plastic zip-loc bag kept it clean and dry – and tempting too. Henry picked it up and removed the sandwich without noticing the slight glint of reflected sunlight or the clear monofilament line that led mysteriously into the sloshing surf.

His first bite was greeted with a sudden yank followed by a sharp stinging pain as a large fishhook sunk deep into the roof of his mouth. Henry was ripped from his lucky spot at the end of the jetty; his flailing body towed down through the sloshing surf. In a more than ironic twist Henry disappeared into the briny deep from what can best be described as a fitting act of piscatorial vengeance.

3

ZENO'S PARADOX

When he finally woke up Michael found himself tied to a large oak tree on the edge of a field in the middle of nowhere. His head felt groggy, his vision moved in and out of focus, and the chilly morning air made him wish that his shirt and his football jacket weren't lying crumpled on the ground. It was probably best that he couldn't see the bullseye that was painted on his bare chest, at least not yet. First string linebacker muscles bulging he struggled mightily against the zip-ties and ropes that bound his wrists and ankles to the tree; his screams for help proved to be just as futile as his attempt to escape.

An older gentleman slowly emerged from the woods, and although Michael thought he looked familiar, he could not place him until he spoke. "Good morning, I'm pleased that you could make it Michael."

A shiver of apprehension pulsed down his spine and the object in the man's red right hand turned that feeling of dread into abject horror.

Then it clicked. It was the man's deep baritone voice and precisely articulated speech. That was it, his best friend's brother's graduation party the night before. It was all coming back to him. It started with small talk that led to a rambling lecture-like discussion about meta-something, yes, metaphysics that was it. The older man was a professor of philosophy and his one-way conversation had left him bored and nodding his head just to appease the guy. Michael's sudden attempt at disengaging led to the professor's insistence that he wasn't quite done. Michael was adamant, "I gotta' pee old man. I'll be back," he said, with no intention of doing so. "A house full of good-looking cheerleaders and I'm stuck listening to a metaphysics lecture," he grumbled to himself as he entered the bathroom. Standing at the toilet he wondered just how he would shake this overly persistent professor.

The rest of the night was just a blur.

The morning found him begging desperately to be untied.

"Oh, no, no, no – not just yet Mike. We have to test an old paradox first."

The professor strode away from Michael stopping at a white wooden stake stuck firmly in the ground. He carefully notched a broadhead arrow into his Annihilator crossbow. Then some minor adjustments while peering through his weapon's rangefinder scope. "Sixty feet on the nose. Not to worry young man, metaphysics is more of an exact science than most are led to believe. I don't expect you to remember my lecture, that was no ordinary drink you know."

"Paradox? Lecture? What are you talking about?" he gasped while yanking hard against his restraints.

"Calm down Michael and show a little faith in my expertise. You jocks are all the same. Muscles where your brains ought to be."

"How can I be calm when you have me tied to a tree and you're standing there holding a loaded crossbow?" It was then that Michael looked down at his bare chest and completely lost it.

"Shhhh. Please. Let me explain. According to Zeno's Achilles Paradox this arrow can't possibly harm you. In fact it will never even reach that target I painted on your chest."

"Wha? What the . . . Zeno? Achilles? You're insane!" Michael shouted at the top of his lungs; and he began to shake uncontrollably. "And why me?"

"If only you showed a little more faith in my academic training and superior intellect. If only you had shown a little more curiosity about metaphysics Michael."

The professor lowered his crossbow and ambled back toward his living target.

"There's no need to worry Mikey; just calm down, listen carefully, and relax and maybe you'll learn that thought experiments have their limits," the professor stated matter-of-factly.

"According to Zeno's Paradox the arrow will never reach you because it must first travel 30 feet on its way to the target on your chest that's 60 feet away. That's half the distance from where I'll be standing. Then it must travel 15 feet — that's half of the remaining distance to the bullseye. Then 7.5 feet — again, half of the remaining distance. And so on, and son, and so on. The arrow must always travel half the remaining distance before it reaches its target and there are an infinite number of half distances, albeit they get quite small by actual measure. Therefore, my young man, this arrow can never reach you."

The professor returned to his mark, raised his loaded Annihilator crossbow, closed his left eye while looking into the scope with his right. "Sixty feet, zero inches," he announced. " And remember, if you move even just the slightest bit, you'll inadvertently alter the target distance."

"Ina, inadvert . . . huh?" stuttered Michael. And he quickly drew a deep breath holding perfectly still just before the professor released the broadhead.

"Practice makes perfect," grinned the professor as a squirrel fell from the tree. The razor sharp broadhead shaft had passed half-way through the lifeless carcass. "I knew that little bugger couldn't hold still. See what I mean Michael." He held up the arrow looking every bit like some sort of grotesque squirrel shish kebab.

"My academic logic is flawless," he announced before slowly notching a second broadhead. The professor adjusted his distance and reminded his new acquaintance, "The tip of my arrow is precisely sixty feet to that bullseye. Now be still, won't you Mike?"

The deep baritone voice provided his exact location with GPS coordinates, followed by a precisely articulated scene report. Before the 911 dispatcher could finish her next question the call abruptly ended with what sounded like a muffled gunshot.

The Life-Flight paramedics thought they had seen it all. They found the unconscious young man pinned to an oak tree by a bloodied broadhead arrow that passed clean through his right pectoral muscle, through his back, and into the trunk. The arrow struck the dead center of the target drawn on his chest with his nipple taking the place of the bullseye. They worked quickly but carefully, stabilizing the wounded man in the Stokes basket before transporting him into the chopper. Just before takeoff, the two paramedics loaded a weighty cadaver pouch alongside their patient. Over the whirr of the rotor, Michael mumbled through a morphine haze, "Wha, what . . . what' . . . s in tha . . . that, b-b-bla . . . b-b-black, bag . . .no . . . who . . . who' . . . sinit . . .?"

Michael eventually made a full recovery and the large X-shaped scar on his right pec became quite the conversation piece – in the locker room – and especially at the town the pool. "So much for metaphysics and Zeno's whatever. A total load of bull-crap if you ask me," became his standard line every time he ended his harrowing tale.

And in a simple twist of fate, that scar led to a first date with the new lifeguard he had his eye on. And that first date led to a happy and enduring marriage with a house filled with three kids who never stopped asking, "Tell us that arrow story again Dad."

4

REVELATIONS

The Voice Recording

My name is Jack Henderson and the truth that my wife Diane and I have uncovered absolutely must be heard. It's a surreptitious lie and we've all been duped. It's a revelation so outlandish that I now doubt most of what our government has been telling us. I've been forced to hold onto it for twenty years, but much, much better late – than never. First, a bit of backstory for context and posterity. You must listen to the entirety of this message, but be forewarned, you do so at your own risk if you decide to copy this and pass it on. Diane and I remain hopeful that you will do the right thing.

The Thermo-Nuclear Conflagration of 2056

During the Thermo-Nuclear Conflagration of 2056, Earth's population was decimated, and much of its surface was reduced to a radioactive wasteland. It took many decades for the human race to fully recover from near extinction. Thanks to some critical foresight, many of our best technical experts, scientists, engineers, doctors, architects, construction specialists, and teachers were protected in our array of Strategic Nuclear Bunkers. This allowed the Global

Governing Body to develop a series of technologies required for adaptation in a world ravaged by nuclear war. Hence, four critical Interventions were developed to salvage human existence. It took over a century to tweak and fine tune these programs as Earth's population rebounded and endemic radiation sickness and widespread starvation were ended. Now that we're over 250 years into the post-apocalyptic era, humans are once again thriving.

Genetic Interventions

The first of the Interventions ushered in mandatory genetic profiling, intensive genetic engineering, along with selective breeding practices that were essential to the rebuilding of critical human resources. Genetic profiling has been used to arrange marriages, to select candidates for Interplanetary Colonization, and it is the key to making successful matches that have made the Rejuvenation Intervention so successful. Genetic engineering has done much to improve the human condition as greed, hatred, distrust, and even curiosity have been nearly eliminated.

Nutra-Blast

For many decades, radioactive fallout proved catastrophic to all prewar food production technologies. The government was forced to develop a successful Nutrition Intervention during the postwar era. This was implemented on the grandest scale as it had to create food supplies for the nearly one billion survivors of the Nuclear Conflagration of 2056. Nutra-Blast is the result, and it still provides all the nutrients we need to live long and healthy lives. Although it comes in different forms with nearly unlimited cooking options and treatments, Nutra-Blast manufacturers can only produce two flavors. Umami is a robust, savory, meaty concoction that is sublimely delicious. Sweet 'n Sour, is a culinary treat that is the perfect complement to Umami. Together, they satisfy the taste palate of humans everywhere; and so delicious, that no one ever complains.

Interplanetary Colonization

The Interplanetary Colonization Intervention was allegedly developed to ensure that the human race would prevail, beyond a damaged Earth and under any unforeseen consequences produced by near nuclear annihilation. When our youngest son, Adam turned 20, the genetic profiling program selected him as an ideal candidate for the third Martian Settlement on the Hellas Planitia impact basin. It was considered an honor for any 20-year-old to be selected for this astronaut training and permanent deployment. At the time, watching his group lift off on Launch Day filled us with great pride. Had we only known then what we know now, those feelings would be more akin to outrage. To make matters worse, Adam is our twenty-third offspring who has been placed into the so-called Interplanetary Colonization program.

The Rejuvenations

The Rejuvenation Initiative is a body exchange program that provides physical and intellectual restoration for all who qualify. The Global Governing Body requires seven, 20-year Rejuvenations starting at age 40, after which there is mandatory retirement from terrestrial society. Receiving young healthy bodies has allowed our minds and souls to spend our extended lives making long-term contributions in our fields of expertise. There is a strict focus on the retention and dissemination of institutional knowledge and wisdom that benefits all generations. The Rejuvenations have produced a very successful selective breeding program as indefinite female fertility has its obvious advantages when the best mothers are identified through genetic profiling. For select parents like us, the government birthing requirement was a minimum of 32 offspring. Not as hard as it sounds when you get seven extra 20-year-old bodies, although my wife might disagree with me.

A Revelation

When Diane and I emerged from our Rejuvenation Pods for the seventh and last time, she stood slack-jawed, shaking her head in shock. One look in the mirror and I understood why. I calmed her down by insisting it had to be a Doppelganger, because my new 20-year-old body was a dead-ringer for our son Adam. We immediately attempted to confirm that it wasn't him, but our uncertainty was intensified by a failed tele-communication session with Adam. We contacted Martian Colonization Headquarters to ask about the voice distortion and the and the herky-jerky, pixelated images. We were met with the usual bureaucratic run-around from Technical Support, but they assured us that they would correct the problem asap. That's when we overheard the team leader on his 'hot mic' – and that's when we discovered the horrible truth. I can still hear his words in my head like the day it happened.

"Jeez, that was a close call Emily – way too close. Get Adam's AI program fixed pronto, or your career is toast. And while you're at, notify the authorities about these Hendersons, they're a bit too nosey for my liking."

Genetic engineering and selective breeding programs have left humans mindlessly accepting an endless supply of young, healthy bodies for the Rejuvenations. Luckily, I didn't need curiosity to figure this out; that "hot mic" transmission was all it took.

No words haunt me more than those I uttered that day. "My god Diane, look at me – this *is* Adam! It's our boy!" It was the moment we both realized that my new body was no Doppelganger; that there are no colonies on Mars or any other planet. And that it was all just a ruse – an AI generated cover for the Rejuvenations!

And of course, it led to obvious complications when it came to romance, especially from Diane's standpoint. Technically it isn't incestual, and besides we had no choice but to follow government regulations. Try as we might, we never did get used to it.

Anyway, my complaint and the suspicion it generated had the two of us red-flagged for round the clock, government surveillance.

Getting this phone after all these years was no easy feat. Getting this to those who need to know will be even harder, but I am determined to make it happen.

Way Down, Below The Ocean, Where We're Sent To Be . . .

Our last twenty years have been very difficult; stressful to say the least. Diane and I are at the end of our final Rejuvenation, and so, our long and productive, but temporary, brush with immortality ended last week. The seventh and final Rejuvenation period ends at age forty, and so it is retirement time. As Eastern Elders, we are about to be transported to the Atlantis Subsurface Retirement Community. Global Governing Rejuvenation Law prohibits any contact with terrestrial Earth, getting this voice recording to those who need to know hinges on the success of my rather risky plan. Fingers crossed.

Our final 40th birthday party was a traditional send-off that neither of us looked forward to as the sight of Adam's now 40-year-old body left us disturbed and disillusioned – yet even more determined to let the world know. The celebration of 180 years well spent in eight different young, healthy bodies had lost all meaning for me and Diane.

As I speak, the Atlantis Subsurface Retirement Community lies just ahead, and we can see submersibles filled with Eastern Elders in a line of undersea traffic.

Diane and I are now disembarking from our craft through the water-tight transfer dock at what promises to be our final, but spec-tacular new home on the ocean floor.

The Dining Halls

We are now being herded onto a mechanical walkway. They've sorted us by gender, I'm in a group of maybe two hundred Elder men; Diane is on a parallel conveyor packed with Elder women. It looks like we're headed for the Dining Halls. We are advancing toward the door labeled, UMAMI MEALS. Elder women are moving slowly toward SWEET 'n SOUR MEALS . We are closing in now, I find Diane, and give a quick wave to get her attention, I mouth the words, "See you soon Dee – I love you."

Not So Savory

Entering the dining hall, the delicious scent of savory umami is wafting over us . . . but I sense that . . . something is not quite . . ., I feel strange, . . . suddenly tired . . . lethargic, weak, . . . many . . . Elder men . . . collapsing . . . heavy eyes . . . short of . . breath . . . not sure how much longer . . . My god . . . this is no, . . . no dining . . . not feeding us, it's . . . ("Click")

Fitzsimmons turns off the phone, a bit shaken, but alerted by what he had just heard.

"Smitty, you know government issued phones are confiscated before all Elder shipments, any idea how this joker got a burner?"

"No idea boss. Good thing I caught him on the conveyor before he hit the Slicing station. Stopped the line for a bit – I literally had to pry that phone from his cold, dead hand."

"Lucky for us. I'll notify the authorities asap – hopefully he was a one-off. Excellent work Smitty, now get back to your Grinding station, that Umami Nutra-Blast sure isn't gonna' make itself."

5

A HELLUVA BARGAIN

Sean Smith thought of himself as a typical screw-up. Probably because he was. Socially awkward, forgetful, bad judgement, bad luck, and being accident prone were all hardwired in his DNA. Having a hot temper didn't help. Quite a cross to bear when you think about it. Sean had one of those dark clouds that seem to follow some people around. And, "had" is the operative word in this cautionary tale. His new mistake-free life came in the form of an app that mysteriously appeared on his phone after an operating systems update. It came uploaded, good to go. No need to, "Get."

Undo

When he opened the app . . .

<u>INSTRUCTIONS</u>
Set: *TIME REVERSAL – Click: UNDO
(*MAX: 10 MIN)

<u>WARNING</u>
Original actions permanently deleted
No do-overs or Re-dos permitted
FOR PERSONAL USE ONLY!

<u>IMPORTANT NOTICE</u>
SEAN, you have qualified for a **FREE**, **ONE YEAR** trial period.
PAYMENT REQUIRED to extend App to "LIFETIME SERVICE"
ALL SALES ARE FINAL
,NO CANCELLATIONS – NO REFUNDS – NO EXCUSES

The app kept track of every "Undo" action initiated.

By the end of the first year, Sean's list was quite impressive.

247 scratch-off losses, 176 fairway irons, 172 text messages, 121 golf drives, 75 work mistakes, 62 golf putts, 48 racetrack bets, 42 over-cooked food items, 39 impulsive decisions, 29 failed pick-up lines, 23 assorted spills, 17 obvious lies, 12 finger cuts, 11 bunker shots, 11 burned food items, 9 clothing stains, 6 shaving nicks, 5 inappro-priate jokes, 4 splinters, 4 all-in poker losses, 3 broken drink glasses, 3 speed trap tickets, 2 you broke, you bought its, 2 severe lacera-tions, 2 fender benders, 2 deer collisions, 2 DUIs, 2 dropped cartons of eggs, 1 broken hand, 1 ground wasp attack, 1 ladder fall, 1 rollover/asleep at the wheel, 1 sprained ankle , 1 lightning strike, 1 circular saw accident, 1 hole-in-one.

Perusing his record of Undo actions left Sean more than satisfied. That mysterious, magical Undo app was like a gift from heaven for a natural born screw-up like himself. It saved him a world of hurt and embarrassment – and a lot of money too. Sean tried, just once, to repeat what he considered to be one of his crowning achieve-ments. It was a dream come true, and he did it on his first swing! A real-life replay would have felt so good. He just had to see the look on his golf buddies' faces again and he just had to feel that exhilaration one more time. But once his first ever hole-in-one was undone, it was gone for good. It wasn't *as if* it never happened – it never did. Forgetting the warning was one big mistake that he could not undo. One that haunted him for a long time and a feeling he had not felt for nearly an entire year.

Sean received a text the night his Undo app service was set to expire.

> Send "YES" to extend your Undo App for "Lifetime Service"
> Payment made through our Barter Program.
> Your ONE and ONLY opportunity to RE-UP.
> *It's a Helluva Bargain Sean!*

He typed, YES – and pressed SEND.

Little did he know, but it would be his very last screw up.

The return text arrived immediately.

> Lifetime Undo App service approved. Sending an email receipt.
> Thank you for your patronage, Sean. – B. Elzebub

He smiled and thought to himself, this is too good to be true.

As he would soon find out, it was really too true to be good.

And then . . . Sean went right to his Inbox . . .

Receipt

B. Elzebub Barter Program

Customer
Sean Smith

No.	Item	Unit Price
1	Lifetime Undo App Service	Your Soul

Paid in Full

A Helluva Bargain!

NO REFUNDS

6

UNBEARABLE GUILT

Sometimes when life comes at you hard, it shows you no mercy. What follows is a recounting of a downward spiral for the ages; one that has left me with unbearable and unrelenting guilt.

It started out as an ordinary Tuesday morning, until it wasn't. Looking back, I picture my wife Sandy standing at the bathroom mirror, brushing her teeth and thinking about the day ahead, completely unaware that Monday was soon going to become the last ordinary day of her life.

In a horrible home accident, Sandy slipped and fell down a full flight of stairs. Two broken ribs, a dislocated shoulder, a compressed spinal disc, and a nearly fatal brain bleed. At the time, I thought she was lucky to be alive.

Not long after her accident we got some unexpected news; Sandy was pregnant. Miraculously, her fall and injuries did not result in a miscarriage. And so, we were left with a wild mix of emotions, a schedule of surgeries, and our first baby on the way.

Complications from her final surgery left Sandy with chronic discomfort and bouts of intense pain. We were assured that short-term use of opioids for pain managementduring her pregnancy would not endanger our child. Her flashes of severe pain became more and more frequent and were, over time, mismanaged by her well-meaning OB GYN. Morphine and fentanyl mainly. It was a chaotic and stressful time. I'm embarrassed to say that we all missed Sandy's transition to self-medication via heroin.

She hid her heroin use with a cunning and guile that all addicts seem to muster. It was discovered only when our daughter was born with neonatal abstinence syndrome. Baby Chloe, like her mother, was a heroin addict. Crying, fever, irritability, seizures, tremors, vomiting and intractable diarrhea. Sadly, the best efforts of the PICU team were not enough. It was a traumatic experience that left my wife with a debilitating swirl of emotions, not the least of which was unbearable guilt.

Sandy's guilt trip took her on a wildly toxic ride of substance abuse. It was a hallucinatory drug-addled fever dream that drove a bloody murder attempt gone bad. Sadly, her OB GYN has been permanently disabled and still suffers from severe PTSD. My wife followed her violent rampage with a botched attempt to take her own life. Sandy is now on suicide watch in the psychiatric ward of Bellevue Hospital here in New York City. Only a few bus stops on the M15 away from our town house on the Lower East Side. I visit her often but have not had the courage to tell her that it was all my fault.

Like I said, a downward spiral for the ages.

And it all started with a single stray dryer sheet.

A dryer sheet at the top of the stairs that my wife didn't notice; probably hidden by the loaded laundry basket she was carrying.

A dryer sheet that I hurried by on my rush to get to work. *Can't be late again for another important meeting. Sandy will get it,* I thought to myself as I rushed out the door.

Little did I know just how bad she would get it.

I've learned the hard way that there are dryer sheets everywhere. They may not look like the one my wife slipped on but they are out there. Often hiding in plain sight. So, when *you* see one, please, I urge you to pick it up. I'll never forgive myself for not taking a few seconds to do just that.

7

IT'S ME

Brian G
Did you guys hear about this? He was 64 –
our age group. Any idea who it is?

Frank P
No idea. I have a hunch we'll recognize his
name when they release it.

Brian G
My thoughts as well

Jim D
Have no heard about this accident

Frank P
I'll send you the article

I don't think he knew what hit him

                                        Phil B
                                        Hey guys, it's me

Brian G
You know we can see your name.

Phil B
I know that

I'm the guy in the article

Frank P
Ha Ha Ha Ha !!!!

Phil B
No, seriously I never felt a thing

and its all good here

no worries

Jim D
You shouldn't be joking about this Phil

Phil B
No joke

I'm dead serious guys

Phil B
Literally

Brian G
Not funny at all

Phil B
Beats showing up as a cardinal at my wake, no?

Frank P
Is it heaven?

Phil B
We don't call it anything

No words can describe it

Brian G
Huh?

Phil B
It's like colors that have no names but they're senses, feelings

Jim D
Crowded?

Phil B
You don't get it

Not a concept here

Brian G
You seem good?

How'd you hang onto your phone

Phil B
I didn't

Frank P
Spookin' me philip

Phil B
Earthbound life is a starting point

Its like a launch pad

Phil B
Physical bodies are just baggage for the soul

Jim D
You're getting weird

Phil B
When you think you've lost a loved one

It's just the opposite

Phil B
Just like I lost all of you

But not forever

Brian G
Ok Phil, had your fun?

Frank P
Enough is enough

Time to give it a break

Jim D
Your creeping me out man

Phil B
Sending a pic for you doubters

Frank P
Can't be real

Brian G
No freaking way

Jim D
Obviously AI

Phil B
Nope. Take a closer look

Frank P
OMG!

Phil B
Bingo!

Later boys

8

ADDICTED

I'm so tired of everyone getting in my face telling me that I'm addicted. Teachers, parents, even my older brother. No way I thought, after all I'm only 13 just doing my thing really. And now my best friend Alicia is telling me that I'm an addict. But I just wanna be me. I'm not hurting anyone. She finally convinced me to Google it. So, I typed: "symptoms of addiction" – and I'm not happy that I did. Dang! I check every box. Yes, to all.

I can't stop doing it or thinking about it when I'm not. Yes, it's affecting my schoolwork. Grades are down and I don't even care. Losing friends and making enemies and all I can do is go back to what caused the problem. Tired of being called an addict. I feel much better when I'm alone with no one bothering me. Trouble sleeping, check! Sometimes not until one or two in the morning. Secretive – check. Including the little white lies to cover it up. When I try to cut back, I get anxious, depressed, irritable, and even angry. So that doesn't last long. Before I know it I'm back at it. I need it just to feel functional, to feel like I'm whole. But as they say, denial is not just a river in Egypt. I finally told Alicia that she may be right, but I don't know what to do or how to stop. I can't stop. I know I need help. Funny thing, I don't want any.

I guess all the warning signs were there. Someone must have reported me because I had to meet with my school's CP addiction counselor. He also happened to be my science teacher, which I was cool with, at first.

When I entered his office, he asked me to close the door and take a seat. After some small talk the questions got real and right to the point. And then he insults me. Tells me I'm no different than the Monarch caterpillars he had in class. That I'm in my own kinda cocoon. Isolated and oblivious. He called it a cyber-cocoon. And I'm like, huh? Then he says something about the "lure of the internet." How it's mad powerful. Stronger than willpower.

Then he gives me the bad news. I have an internet addiction. Tells me I'm at Defcon 2 – whatever that means.

The good news was, he could help me. So, he puts me into his 4-Step Program. Tells me it's a no-nonsense approach, just what I need. No new age mumbo-jumbo, no touchy feely crapola, no preachy lectures. He says it starts right here. and right now.

I did what he asked, even though I told him I didn't trust him. I sat there staring at the floor, wondering what the first step in his program was gonna be. I'd heard about 12-step programs, so I was just glad this was gonna be shorter. Didn't realize just how short it would be.

He stood up, walked over to it, and he stepped on it three times. Hard. Smashed it to pieces.

I cringed at the sound of it.

"That's three steps," he said, "The fourth step, Maria, is to get a life."

I looked down in horror at the pieces of plastic and glass scattered across his office floor.

I was so mad I wanted to hit him. I screamed instead, "Get a life? Get a life? How can I get a life now that you wrecked my phone!"

9

LAST WORDS

My name is Michael Kelly, and I have had plenty of time to reflect on how we got here. The movement that I have become an unwilling participant in is a case of social justice gone mad. I'm convinced that it was the 2024 murder of UnitedHealthcare CEO Brian Thompson that caused the tectonic shift. A cultural tsunami that washed over our fundamental beliefs in jurisprudence. And it started with the justification of the murder and the lionization of the alleged killer – on of all things – moral grounds. Chants of "Free Luigi," 70,000 laughing emojis, and a spontaneous SNL ovation were just a few pieces of the puzzle that turned an accused, cold-blooded assassin into a 21st century folk-hero.

The fate that awaits me was foreshadowed over 15 years ago by road signs that appeared in the wake of Brian Thompson's murder: ONE LESS CEO – MANY MORE TO GO!

Tomorrow I will spend my last hours in the visitor's locker room of the arena. I will be wearing my corporate CEO uniform: Brunello Cucinelli Super 150 suit, black Oxfords by Alfred Sargent, Patek Philippe Celestial watch, and a decidedly non-corporate set of Smith and Wesson black hinged handcuffs along with complimentary leg irons. All six of us will be wearing black leather ball-type, gag masks while we wait our turn. Operations protocol requires us to be strapped to a backboard if non-compliant. I'll do my best to face it like a man.

My crime against humanity was being the Chief Executive Officer of the last global energy corporation to promote the combustion of fossil fuels. Evidence against me included, the accelerated melting of the Arctic and Antarctic ice sheets, an average rise of nearly 1.5 meters in ocean levels, the widespread collapse of critical ecosystems, and the over 270 million heat related deaths over the past decade.

Tomorrow at noon I will be led onto the center stage of the arena. Three of my grandchildren will be there in my family's VIP box cheering and jeering along with a throng of 20,000 spectators waiting to lead the countdown.

The heavy stainless-steel blade of the stainless-steel guillotine will be raised to a height of 33 meters producing an impact speed of 55 miles per hour after spending 2.5 seconds in nearly frictionless freefall. My properly coiffed head will fall into a crystal-clear polycarbonate container and then sold at auction. Four Jumbotron screens will allow for prime viewing and slow-motion replays. This is the third annual Social Justice Gala, and it will be live streamed to millions of homes world-wide.

The state-of-the-art Sphere Immersing 3-D sound system will present my final message with perfect clarity. I have chosen my last words very carefully.

After the arena emptied the six VIP groups were escorted from their luxury boxes down to the main stage for the viewing. Blood still dripped from the blade adding to the concoction of human gore in the catch bucket. The six trophies harvested were hosed down and displayed on stainless steel spikes. Brass nameplates identified each of them while 12 vacant eyes stared into rows of empty seats; their carcasses hung from six wooden crosses.

The Kelly entourage formed their reception line when called. They laughed, taking selfies with the family patriarch. A few shot vids for shock-reels. One guest spat in each of their waxen faces. A family friend placed a souvenir in a ziploc bag, and another snickered as she left a burning cigar in a mouth that had no use for it. Michael Kelly's grandchildren were last in line.

Before her brother could start writing, Maureen yanked it from his hand.

"Hey, gimme back my Sharpie!"

"Sean. How *dare* you!"

"Come on Mo, just trying to have some fun. The old man's big bald head was begging for it. Might drive up the bidding too."

"Gross. Didn't you hear his last words? He was pointing at *us*."

"Nah. Me and Jamesie were too busy booin'. The crowd nearly drowned the old man out. Besides, how dare he leave us a world on fire."

The auctioneers arrived as the Kellys were getting ready to leave. As they wheeled six cryogenic shipping canisters onto the stage, James gave them a big thumbs-up and a loud, "Ka-ching baby!"

On their limo ride back to Greenwich, Sean's curiosity got the best of him. "So, what were they Mo? Can't imagine that ecological criminal had anything good to say."

"Not what I expected," said Maureen.

"Well? You're not gonna' leave us hangin' are you?" asked Sean.

"Why not hear it from him?" Maureen replied, "It's already up on YouTube."

James held up his phone as the three of them watched their Grampa address the crowd.

"Well ladies and gentlemen, your third annual Social Justice Gala is almost over. You have come here to this modern-day Colosseum to celebrate cruelty and vengeance. This spectacle comes courtesy of the strongest force in human nature – the overwhelming power of unfettered emotions. Today, morality, virtue, and rational thought are the real victims. The six of us are just collateral damage." After a long pause and a glance skyward, he continued, "Father, please forgive them for they know not what they do."

Then, Michael Kelly pointed at his luxury box eyes fixed on his grandchildren. His voice cracked as he spoke, "I love you all, more than words can say. Now it's time to bid you fare-thee-well."

Then he nodded to the burly blood splattered man in the black hood, "Let's do it."

10

UNMISTAKABLE SOUNDS

Leonard's wife Viktoria interrupted his afternoon nap when she turned on the vacuum.

"Lenny, you up?"

"Yeah. No thanks to that vacuum cleaner. You know I hated that noise ever since I was kid."

"Did you spill something on the side of the couch?"

"Don't think so"

"Take a look. Funny, it looks familiar."

"Familiar?"

"Like Shaggy's drool."

"Viki, I asked you not to mention him. You know. Especially today."

"Today?"

"You never could remember his birthday, could you."

Leonard loved Shaggy like no other dog. He was a rescue. The goofiest, most good-natured dog ever. *His* dog. The Shagster. Shaggy-doo. Shagg-man. Full bread Newf. Even had his papers.

Lenny still hadn't gotten over his passing one year ago. Left a hole in his heart that he thought would never heal.

Lenny took a look at the couch.

"Son of a gun Vik, it sure does look familiar. Slimy. Smells too. Looks like his drool. Feels like his drool. And smells like his drool. Damn. Shaggy slime if I didn't know better."

Later that night Victoria noticed her husband fussing in the pantry.

"Leonard D. Martin, what on earth are you doing?"

"Nothin'."

"I only wish it was nothin'. You haveta' be kiddin' me. That goo on the couch make you lose your mind Lenny?"

"Figured it couldn't hurt." And he stifled a sob while rubbing his reddened eyes.

"Couldn't hurt? The straight jacket you might wind up in sure could."

"What's the worst that can happen Vik?"

"Men with the straight jacket knockin' on our door?"

"No, seriously."

"If it makes you happy, I'm not gonna stop you. I'm goin' to bed, you comin' up?"

"Soon enough."

Lenny placed Shaggy's water bowl right next to his food bowl in his old familiar spot. And they were both full.

Leonard was a sound sleeper. Normally. Later that night he woke up and checked his phone.

11:44

"Lenny? You up? Something buggin' you?"

"Yeah Vik. You know."

"Forget it Len. Get back to sleep. You'll feel better in the morning."

"Viki! Listen. Shhhhh. Do you hear that?"

"Hear what?"

"It sounds just like . . "

"Your hearing things Len," interrupted Viktoria, "Now get some shut eye, huh."

But Leonard heard it loud and clear. The sound was unmistakable. A sound he had listened to every night for over 12 years. Crunching nuggets. Then the lapping. Shaggy washing down his dinner. Impossible, thought Leonard, must be the pipes.

———————✦———————

11:50

"Lenny, where on god's green earth are you going at this hour?"

"I'll be right back."

"Back? Back from where?"

"Just wanna check on that noise Vik."

"You were probably just dreamin'. Come on back to bed."

He could still hear it as he walked down the hallway. Then it stopped. As he headed downstairs he heard another unmistakable sound, a jingling, jangling chain. Same sound for 12 years. It sent a chill right through him.

He knew he wasn't sleepwalking. And he knew that those unmistakable sounds were no dream. Maybe the pipes?

When Leonard Martin turned on the kitchen light, what he saw in the mudroom stopped him dead in his tracks.

"Shaggy? That you?"

And there stood his old dog, looking young and spunky. Big smile. Leash in his mouth and his tail wagging.

And then the completely unmistakable sound.

"Woof!"

Lenny put on his jacket, slipped into his boots, and grabbed his flashlight.

"Woof, woof!"

Lenny was convinced that he was the only one who could understand Shaggy's different woofs. This was just like old times. He gave him a scratch on the head and an ear rub. The unmistakably delightful groan-growl was still there. Leonard grabbed the leash, hooked him up, opened the back door, and stepped into the night with his best friend at his side.

As they walked down the gravel driveway Shaggy pulled like he was a kid again. While Lenny stopped to let him pee, something bugged him. It was the fog. Thick as pea soup. Turned his flashlight into a lightsaber. *Funny*, he thought, *it was a bright moonlit night earlier. Clear as a bell.*

11:58

Viktoria Martin peered through her bedroom window and rubbed her eyes as if to make it go away. She could have sworn that she just saw Lenny and Shaggy walking side by side as they disappeared into the fog bank at the end of their driveway. "It can't be," she whispered to herself, "Please god, please, this has to be a dream."

Viktoria rushed downstairs in a panic. The kitchen light was still on. She looked down and gasped! A heart-in-the-throat kind of gasp. Nugget crumbs in the bottom of the bowl. A swirl of dog drool floating in the little bit of water that was left. Lenny's jacket and boots were gone. Then it hit her. *That was no dream.*

12:00 am

She ran out the door.

Moonlight shining brightly. Clear as a bell. Viki screamed into the empty night.

"LENNY!...LENNY!!!...NO!!!"

11

MY SENTENCE

My name is Derek Peterson, and I am in the twentieth year of a life sentence with no chance of parole. However, I have not spent a single day behind bars; not a minute on death row where I belong. Instead, my punishment is infinitely worse than physical incarceration. Not even solitary could compare with what I have been forced to endure. Now that I have your attention, a little bit about how I got here . . .

It would be too easy to blame my violent nature on the physical abuse I experienced as a child, or the relentless bullying from my classmates in public school. In retrospect, I have no one to blame but Dr. Brian Broca. That nitpicking old codger would still be alive today if only he had the sense to look the other way during my PICU rotation. If only that old fool had let my slip-up slide I would have moved on, aced my medical boards, and walked into a six, maybe seven figure future. Instead, I was tracked into the last group of violent criminals subjected to psychological incarceration.

I can still remember, as if it happened yesterday, waking up in the recovery room with a row of 8 stainless-steel staples on each side of my shaved head. Lurking below those shiny surgical closures, deep in the medial temporal lobe of my brain, is a technology designed to inflict a form of criminal punishment that, at the time, many prophetically called "too cruel and too unusual." The surgeons just called them what they were: ENIs – electronic neural implants. In my case, a set of four chips precisely located in key areas of the limbic system of my brain.

Our psychological sentences were programmed to meet the severity of our offenses. The cruel and sadistic nature of my crime and my complete lack of remorse resulted in the harshest sentence allowable by law. Can you guess which emotion I have been sentenced to endure forever?

To say the least, things did not go well for psychological penal reform. Midway through that experimental year, ENI policy makers were forced to de-program for suicidal ideations. After one year, ENI sentencing was abolished due to the inhumanity of the policy. The punitive manipulation of human emotions is now considered a form of torture, and the original ENI program is still considered one of the darkest periods in the history of American jurisprudence.

For those of us who were sentenced under this policy there was no chance of a reprieve as the extreme nature of our emotional over-load was deemed far too valuable to the scientific community. Thanks to us guinea pigs, advances in positive emotional control technologies are providing unlimited benefits to people everywhere. It's ironic that a handful of irredeemable criminals are unable to feel the redemption we earned the hard way.

———————————*———————————

Prior to my medical indiscretion, I would occasionally see a driver crying in their car. I felt zero sympathy, but did objectively wonder what could produce such a display of emotion. In a strange and twisted way this analysis helped fuel many of my sadistic fantasies. Could it be a romantic break up or the sudden end of a marriage? The tragic death of a loved one always seemed likely. Maybe they were driving the family dog to the vet to be euthanized? One never really knows what personal tragedy caused those tears to flow.

Regardless, the focal point of such heartache is almost always the result of some kind of deeply emotional loss. It always made me thankful that my psychosis made it impossible to feel anything, much less gut-wrenching sadness and grief. Little did I know that it would change forever thanks to that prissy old tattle tale Dr. Brian Broca.

Over the two decades since my sentencing, I've stopped at countless stoplights and have been caught in many traffic jams. There's something about driving alone in my car; it remains the one place outside my home where the pain of constant sorrow physically overwhelms me. I think of all of the people who have noticed me crying and have been left wondering what horrible emotional loss I was struggling through. Little could they guess that my eternal, gut-wrenching grief is a prison that I can never escape from.

So, if you find yourself in the grip of profound and unrelenting sadness, maybe crying alone in *your* car, take some solace in knowing that your grief is not a life sentence. The wait is never easy, but time will eventually soften your sadness and ease your anguish. I wish you well on your journey to healing.

12

ALIEN FREAK SHOW

When Lilliana got home from her sub-orbital instruction pod, she could not contain her excitement. The 174th annual, Old Tyme Carnival was in town; a relic from the distant past that was a step back in time. All her friends were talking about it and those who had been there described the fun and excitement of the rides, the food, the exhibits, and the games with amazing, old-school prizes. But the biggest buzz was about the newest attraction – the Alien Freak Show. The only must-see feature at this year's Carnival was a welcome break from the same-old, same-old. Freakish looking creatures supposedly from a different galaxy. Those who hadn't yet made the visit listened spellbound, finding the stories about the alien freaks almost too hard to believe. Lillianna had found the annual Old Tyme Carnival to be a little boring now that she was into her late teenage years, but the news of the Alien Freak Show convinced her that this year would be different.

Later that evening, at the dinner table, Lilliana pleaded with her parents to take her to see the Alien Freaks. Her father was as curious as she was and completely fascinated by everything he'd heard from his friends and co-workers. Her mother, not so much. It was an easy and enthusiastic, "Let's do it," as he agreed to a father-daughter night out at the Old Tyme Carnival.

———————•———————

When Lilliana and her father arrived at the fairgrounds they headed straight for the Alien Freak Show. The line was long, but the wait turned out to be more than worth it. After buying their tickets they entered the large tent and found dozens of cages holding alien freaks.

As they moved from cage to cage, they were mesmerized by what they saw. The aliens were all very slight in stature, the biggest could be cradled like a newborn baby and the youngest could be held in the palm of a hand. Their heads were remarkably tiny with faces so horribly disfigured that at first, they were painfully hard to look at. They moved about on oddly configured limbs and their skin and hair had a very odd range of colors. Most of the aliens scurried about quickly and seemed anxious or agitated by the crowds. Some cowered in the corners of their cages while others taunted carnival visitors with odd and unintelligible sounds. One fell into the habit of throwing its strange body excrement at anyone who peered too closely into its cage.

"My gosh, those aliens sure are ugly – so grotesque," her father quipped, "Way more freakish than I imagined. I have no idea how they could possibly survive on their own."

"I don't know Dad, they look kinda' cute if you look at them right, just different."

"Seriously Lil', cute? They're repulsive. And it's not just their appearance. Look how they behave, so uncouth, so uncivilized, so inferior – they're like animals."

It must have been the teenager in her when she decided to challenge her father. "Are they really freaks Dad? Wherever they came from I think they would be considered pretty normal to each other. I bet their family and friends back home never thought of them as freaks."

"Lillianna, you sound a little over-protective of these bizarre little buggers. What gives? Would you really want to have them as class-mates or even living in our neighborhood?"

Lillianna just shook her head thinking, *My Dad the xenophobe, Ugghhh.*

The cages ringed the perimeter of the tent and in the center was a fenced-in area with several dozen aliens milling around. Visitors could toss food to them and were even allowed to briefly hold an alien for an up close and personal experience, and of course, photo ops.

"Oh Daddy please can I cuddle one, they're soooo cute? And can you take a few pics for me?"

Her father agreed, thinking to himself, *Better you than me girl.*

The attendant inside the fence removed one of the younger more docile aliens and handed it to Lilliana. "Be careful and don't squeeze too hard," he advised.

Lilliana held the alien in her arms rocking it like a baby and humming a lullaby from her childhood. When she leaned in to give it a tickle the alien lunged forward sinking its teeth into the tip of her finger – and it wouldn't let go. She let out a shriek and reflex-ively ripped it off with her other hand, flinging it to the ground. The young alien crumpled in a heap, emitting what proved to be its final gasp. The body lay limp and lifeless on the hard floor and a puddle of liquid formed around the back of its small, underdeveloped head.

A red light began flashing, accented by a high-pitched beeping. A voice over the loudspeaker called for a clean-up crew at the Center Corral. When they arrived, the men gloved up, placed the alien in biohazard waste bag, and then scrubbed the dark liquid from the concrete floor.

Lilliana apologized effusively, "Oh my! I'm so, so sorry. I just reacted without thinking."

The crew chief said, "Don't worry kiddo, it happens every now and then. Besides, we have plenty of replacements in the back."

Lillianna was more upset than hurt and was left with a few shallow teeth marks on the tip of her finger. After she settled down, the two wrapped up their grand tour of caged alien freaks. And despite the attack on her finger, Lillianna still took their side every time her father made disparaging or inappropriate remarks about the alien freaks.

On their way out they passed by a small, make-shift office and noticed a man working at his desk. They knocked on the open door and were greeted with a big smile and a warm welcome. "Howdy! Name's Xavier but most everyone calls me The X-Man – alien bounty hunter extraordinaire."

Lilliana and her Dad introduced themselves and mentioned just how fascinating the Alien Freak Show was. "Freakier than advertised," complimented her father.

"Cuter than expected," added Lilliana.

"Well, word sure is spreading fast. My export business is booming. You'd be shocked at how popular these little critters have become. I stock alien freak shows all over the place, but it's gotten way bigger than that. Some real creative entrepreneurs out there. Exotic pet stores, game hunting preserves, selective breeders, and death-match fight promoters are all clamoring for more. Alien protein ranches are beginning to crop up as their flesh is supposed to be tender and flavorful; quite the delicacy I hear."

This last thought repulsed Lillianna, and she had trouble hiding her disgust.

"Not your cup of tea, sweetie? That's ok, they're definitely not for everyone. All I can say is, I sell 'em as fast as I can get 'em. A real lucrative fad, if I don't say so," added the X-Man.

"Just one quick question before we go" asked Lillianna's father, "Are they really from another galaxy?"

"Sure are. No secrets here," replied The X-Man, "They were all collected from a rather unremarkable little solar system in the Orion Spur of the Milky Way. We found them on a small rocky, watery planet in a rudimentary stage of development. It's the third one from their Sun and the place is absolutely crawling with them. Got lucky if you ask me – the other eight planets didn't have a sign of life."

13

ONE PIECE AT A TIME

Dr. Stein had been a world-renowned neurosurgeon until early onset Parkinson's disease cut his brilliant career short, right around his 44th birthday. Not one to fold up his tent when faced with a little adversity, he parlayed his declining surgical skills into a job as the county coroner. His hands were still steady enough to remove a liver or lung, and medical bone saws require little skill or training. And so, his improbable second career began.

This particular tale, believe it or not, started with an old Johnny Cash song. After first hearing it on his car radio, Dr. Stein was intrigued enough by the lyrics to download it to his Spotify playlist. *One Piece At a Time* quickly became his personal theme song as the refrain so aptly described his work. His colleagues quickly grew tired of it and started calling him by his first name because it annoyed him as much as his song annoyed them. "Dr. Frank" was a moniker he put up with but didn't particularly care for. It was his last name that reverberated through the neurosurgical profession for nearly a decade with each and every innovative surgical technique or instrument he developed. But through it all, the lyrics of Cash's catchy country tune were stuck in his head for good. But it was the underlying concept that intrigued him the most. And that concept became the source of a somewhat gruesome idea that gave him the intellectual and surgical challenge he needed since being forced to retire so early. And as you can probably guess, it had nothing to do with building a Cadillac.

And so, Dr. Frank Stein began to *acquire* the body parts he needed to complete his personal challenge – one piece at a time. His main source was indigent men without friends or family. He also made use of those scheduled for cremation as a missing part would never be noticed. He completed his surgical work in his home lab, storing his creation between operations in his walk-in freezer.

His laboratory included a well-equipped operating room as it was there that he developed and practiced many of his innovative techniques and procedures – using dogs and pigs mainly. His wife Lisa was a gifted vascular surgeon and became a crucial accomplice in his surreptitious endeavor. She was as excited as he was as their creation slowly took shape.

The Stein's were anxious to test their work at its earliest stage: just a torso and a head. They named their partially complete creation, La'zar – which was short for Lazarus. All they needed was a thunderstorm that featured frequent and violent cloud-to-ground lightning strikes. Bolts with enough super-high voltage to bring their creation to life.

Once the full electrical circuit was completed, from lightning rod to electrodes, it was just a matter of time. When that hot humid summer night finally arrived the Steins carefully attached the electrodes to all of the critical locations on La'zar's thawed-out torso and head.

Then it happened. The crack of the thunder bolt was loud, and the voltage was high. Dr. Stein howled with excitement as La'zar's eyes slowly opened and his chest heaved with the breath of life. He began to speak in an uneven and distorted voice. Poor usage and grammatically confusing at first. It wasn't long before La'zar's language skills were back in full. The two surgeons quickly realized that a walking, talking, sentient, and even emotional human being was close at hand.

Over the course of the night and into the early morning Dr. Stein and his wife were able to converse with La'zar, learning that he had above average intelligence, a strong vocabulary, a relatively pleasant personality, and even a pretty good sense of humor. They wondered if they should announce their amazing achievement immediately. This level of success, they reasoned, was enough to astonish the medical community. La'zar would have been heralded as a living breathing miracle and Dr. Stein would have rocketed to worldwide fame, gaining celebrity status far beyond his old circle of neurosurgeons and their medical journals. "Why take any chances when we have a living breathing talking head to show the world?" he asked Lisa. She shrugged her shoulders in apparent agreement with his rhetorical question.

When La'zar overheard their intentions, he voiced his strong objections. He insisted that Dr. Stein continue as he yearned to be an ordinary, full-bodied human.

"Please Frank, please – Lisa, I'm begging you, I can't just be a talking head, please, I beg you, complete me and together we will astound the world!"

And so, Dr. Stein begrudgingly agreed, placing La'zar back in the deep freeze until he could collect all of the required body parts. The Steins expertise in neurological and vascular microsurgery made the attachment of his extremities seem easy. The sutured connections were nearly impossible to detect from ordinary distances. The real trick was keeping his full body relatively symmetrical despite being composed of many different donors, too dead to know what they were literally a part of.

—————————•—————————

Once La'zar's body was physically complete it was simply a matter of waiting for another violent electrical storm passing through, providing a high-voltage surge that would flow through the full complement of electrodes attached to every critical neurological juncture on his body. And when that moment came, Dr. Stein and his wife got the shock of their lives when La'zar immediately sat bolt upright. Not just alive, but electrically super-charged. "Too much voltage," Stein wondered aloud, "Did I over-do it?"

La'zar sprang off the operating table, pulling electrodes from his naked body. He sprinted across the room and burst through the exterior door with almost superhuman strength. Stein and his wife could hear him shout with joy as he ran outside, "Free at last, free at last thank you Fank Stein, I'm free at last!" They both froze at the sound of a blaring of a car horn and the screeching of tires as they skidded along the road outside their lab – followed by the unmistakable "thunk" of metal colliding with human flesh. An anguished cry of pain – then silence.

The Steins rushed outside and their worst nightmare materialized as lightning bolts lit up the night. La'zar's lifeless body lay in a crumpled heap on the roadway in front of the crushed front end of the vehicle that hit him. And irony of ironies, Johnny Cash's voice, slightly muffled by the airbag, could be heard singing the song that started it all.

Sadly, the living proof of his remarkable neuro-surgical skills and amazing medical creativity was gone. Dead as a doornail. Dr. Frank Stein was beyond distraught and cried out into the dark and stormy night, "I knew it! I knew it! He should have quit while he was a head."

14

NO TIME FOR PATIENCE

"Bless-me-father-for-I-have-sinned-it-has-been-one-month-since-my-last-confession-and-these-are-my-sins."

The priest tried to listen carefully as his penitent continued to race his way through the Sacrament of Reconciliation. Father Flanigan was all too familiar with the litany of venial sins he was hearing. The man on the other side of the screen was one of his regulars. Uncontrollable anger, frustration, irritability, aggression, disrespect, impoliteness, bullying, and constant whining and complaining. He was apparently in too much of a hurry, as he overlooked the one transgression that was the source of all his problems.

Confessionals are designed to honor the privacy of the confessant, but Father Flanigan knew just who he was listening to. Constantly fidgeting in his pew, scrolling manically on his phone. Jumping out of his aisle seat to get to the head of the communion line. Chewing the host. Hurrying out just before the Recessional. And here in the sanctity of the confessional booth, once again, rushing through the sacrament in a rude and frantic manner. Father Flanagan just shook his head, *This fool not only disrespects the Sacrament, but he disrespects Time itself.*

———————————•———————————

Patience is no doubt a virtue, but Johnny Murphy didn't want anything to do with it. His colleagues at work found his impatience rude and annoying. He was a menace on the roads; his car horn blaring the instant a stoplight turned green, racing around school buses, passing on double yellows, and flashing his brights to get you out of his way. Speeding tickets went in the trash. His lawyer asked if it was worth losing his wife, not to mention all the money that it cost him. Johnny's physician urged him to manage his impatience induced frustration and stress before it killed him. Johnny Murphy's stock reply never changed: "You don't get it. I have no time for patience."

———————————•———————————

Ordinary absolution had become enabling, so Father Flanigan decided upon a penance that was, to say the least, highly unusual. A penance that required him to make the most of his affinity for the dark and mystical side of religion. He excused himself from the confessional and returned shortly to the sound of Murphy shouting, "Hey Flanigan, can you move this thing along I don't have all day."

Upon his return, the priest slid open the partition and held a well-worn pocket watch up to the latticed screen. Johnny was struck by the Roman numerals that spiraled down into the clock face, and the unusually rapid cadence of the ticking. Smoke and the pungent odor of incense mixed with a harsh, ungodly voice. Old Latin spoken as if it came from the netherworld instead of Father Flanagan.

"Father? Hey! Is that you?"

"Yes my son, the incantation is complete. And for your penance you must carry this sacred timepiece with you at all times. And you are required to use it as dictated by sacramental law." .

"What do you mean, use it?"

"The next time you're feeling impatient my son, feeling angry and rushed, simply advance the minute hand and you will see. Advance the hour hand too, if you dare. The only real limit will be the finite amount of time you have left here on earth. Never forget that this is your penance and yours alone. The power this hallowed watch bestows upon you is not to be shared with anyone else – nor can it ever be spoken of."

Once he got the hang of it, Johnny Murphy never had to wait again – for anything. Twenty-minute fast food lines became instantaneous meals. Stoplights an eyeblink. Monday mornings became Friday afternoons in no time. The really strange thing about leapfrogging time was that Johnny had memories of everything that occurred in every jump.

At the end of what was an extraordinarily quick year, Johnny Murphy returned to the confessional. Instead of a list of venial sins all he had was a question. "What am I missing, Father? That watch makes time fly. Nothing near atonement. I just don't get it."

"Well, for someone like yourself who does not value the precious gift of time it may seem a blessing for now. One day you may find that rushing through your finite supply is a penance far more severe than reciting a few Hail Marys and Our Fathers. Remember my son, like all of us, you only get so many hours before your allotted time runs out."

Johnny Murphy, the man who had no time for patience was stopped at a railroad crossing. Warning lights flashing; black and white striped gates blocking his path and the sound of the oncoming train in the distance. Impatience was now a thing of the past for Johnny as he confidently began to twist the crown of his pocket watch. After just a tiny fraction of a turn, it suddenly froze, as if some unknown force grabbed it and wouldn't let go. Johnny's final burst of time travel produced a jump of just a few seconds, leaving him stuck waiting, just like the old days. But this time would be different as a furious flash of anger triggered a sudden spike in his blood pressure. His undiagnosed brain aneurysm exploded, right on schedule, delivering the last sensations he would know. Dizziness, blurred vision, vomiting, and what felt like a railroad spike being sledgehammered deep into his brain. It was a fairly quick demise – but not fast enough for him to escape the irony.

As it turned out, Time clearly had no patience for Johnny Murphy.

15

SHOP 'TIL YOU DROP,
THEN BUY 'TIL YOU DIE

Shirley Thompson was consumed with acquiring things. She was the ultimate consumer of material products. Clothing, shoes, handbags, indoor and outdoor furniture, lamps, gym equipment, sculptures, paintings, nicknacks, do-dads, decorations, bed stuff, bath stuff, and beyond stuff. And everything you can imagine for "Cinnamon," her pampered, three-year-old, Best-in-Breed champion Chow-Chow. But those doggie purchases didn't begin to compare with the high-end English horse tack she lavished on her pair of Dutch Warmbloods – and her exclusive collection of fine riding apparel she needed to show them.

Shopping was fun, but buying was better. Tired of the big malls and stores and specialty shops, she spent most of her time buying from home. The world of online purchasing was close to limitless for serial shoppers like Shirley. Not a day went by that a UPS, USPS, or FedEx truck didn't pull into the driveway of her posh and very well-appointed home in her gated community. She was on a first name basis with all the drivers and tipped them well during the holidays.

The joy she got from opening those boxes was unmatched by anything else in her life. Her husband Benjamin more than tolerated the endless string of purchases. "Happy wife – happy life" was his mantra. Since money was not an issue for the wealthy couple, Shirley's mantra was, "I can't take it with me." Unfortunately, no one bothered to tell her that she couldn't take all that stuff with her either.

Her best friend Norma once urged her to think about putting some of their wealth into a charity instead of more stuff, more boxes, more waste – to think about others less fortunate. Shirley laughed at the thought. "Less fortunate? Why Norma my dear, Benjamin has worked very hard to invest the fortune he inherited. Besides, I like to think of myself as a special type of charity. I'm proud to be a material girl, Madonna has nothing on me." When Norma suggested that admitting her greediness might be inviting bad karma, Shirley laughed again, "Bad karma? Seriously Norma, I never did believe in that silly stuff."

On some days the number of boxes delivered was overwhelming – and unsightly. So, Shirley did what she did best – she bought something. Before long a custom built, teak storage shed – the type intended for lawn and garden equipment – was delivered. It looked a little out of place in a gated community where everyone had weekly landscaping and gardening services. Shirley loved the convenience of her beautiful new "delivery shed" and didn't care what her neighbors thought. It was 10 x 10, just the right size to hold the largest delivery of boxes on any given day. Opening the shed in the early morning added to the thrill of the buy, never quite sure what new thing would be waiting for her.

It was a quiet September morning when Shirley opened the shed to find just a single item in the center of the floor. It was a large crate, big enough to fit a good-sized refrigerator. The dozens of holes reminded her of the containers used to ship live animals. It was an unexpected delivery that, for good reason, she did not recognize. As she stretched high up on her tippy toes looking for a shipping label, the shed door suddenly closed behind her. Surrounded in darkness, the smell of rotting flesh rode a wave of hot breath from behind. By the time it reached her, it was too late.

Moments later an 8-wheeler cargo truck slowly pulled into the Thompsons' driveway. Black lettering stood out against the cherry red side panel:

Nether Worldwide-Shipping

The truck parked with the engine running and two very enormous delivery men emerged from the cab. If anyone had seen them, they would have sworn they were looking at two Orcs straight from the mountains of Middle-Earth. They lifted the crate from the shed, loading it onto their truck with ease despite the hefty live weight moving inside it.

The brute of a man riding shotgun returned to the shed with a portable power washer. There was a light red tinge to the water as it drained off the concrete floor and seeped into Shirley's well-manicured lawn. He picked up a fleshy morsel that they apparently overlooked and stuffed it into his shirt pocket, thinking that it would make a nice treat on the long ride back. As he lowered the cargo truck's roll-down door, they could hear the Thing inside the crate slurping, snorting, and belching with delight.

As the truck pulled away, the driver grunted and growled in a barely intelligible dialect, "Shirley sure had it coming. Shame she never learned the best things in life 'aint things."

The creature riding shotgun nodded his enormous, disfigured head in agreement. "Like the Boss always tells us, their world's a better place every time people like her get consumed by one of our Things."

16

DENALI

My name is Karl Reinhold and this story is about the juxtaposition of my remarkable success in defying death and injury and the horrible tragedy that ended it all.

In my former life I was a legendary, world-class athlete who had successfully completed some of the riskiest physical challenges in some of the most dangerous places on Earth. Cave diving the Eagle's Nest Sinkhole in Florida, base jumping Angel Falls in Venezuela, wingsuiting down the Troll Wall in Norway, heli-skiing New Zealand's Southern Alps, big-wave surfing the Peahi Jaws in Maui, and kayaking the Ghostrider rapids on the Zambezi River were all on my life list of danger-filled accomplishments.

In my new life I am now a wheelchair-bound paraplegic, fully paralyzed from the waist down. In a very unfortunate accident, my spine was severed between the T5 and T6 vertebrae. Like most, I never imagined this could happen to me. I am now a burden on my family and society and unable to pursue my passion for outdoor adventure. And I am only 27 years old. I often wish my life had ended when I fell.

My success with high-risk outdoor activities was in large part due to my exceptional physical conditioning along with a wide range of technical skills developed over countless hours of training and practice. But the real secret was my meticulous level of preparation, both mental and physical. I also had my share of very close calls and brushes with death where lady luck always seemed to be on my side. Some say it's better to be lucky than good, but my success in the world of extreme sports required both.

Next on my list was extreme mountain climbing. An ordinary mountain in an ordinary way was never going to be enough to satisfy my desire to try to do what most could not. So, I decided to make a solo ascent of Denali in the dead of winter. It was an accomplishment only 17 others could claim at the time – and six others who died trying. I had hoped that Alaska's extreme conditions would prepare me for my ultimate goal of soloing Mount Everest, in the dead of the Himalaya winter – without oxygen or the assistance of Sherpas.

Denali is the highestmountainpeak inNorth America, located the Alaska Range. It has an elevationof 20,310 feet abovesea level and is the crown jewel of Denali National Park. Summiting Denali requires completing an 18.000-foot, base-to-peak vertical ascent, which no other mountain in the world can match – not even Everest.

Research was an essential step in developing a plan for surviving my climb. I knew I would be facing a harsh, sub-zero arctic winter with icy technical climbs, glacial traverses, hidden crevasses, oxygen deprived elevations, and the isolation of a three-week solo climb with little more than five hours of sunlight per day. Physical, mental, and psychological readiness combined with state-of-the-art technical equipment gave me all the confidence I needed for success.

But back to my new life and how I got here. If you are expecting a harrowing tale of injury and near death on the icy slopes of Denali complete with a dramatic helicopter rescue, you can stop reading now. To call what happened ironic, would be an understatement of the highest order.

After completing my successful climb I flew out of Anchorage with stopovers in Seattle and Chicago before my planned return to my home in Frankfurt, Germany. As Mike Tyson once said, "Everyone has a game plan, until they get punched in the face." Truer words were never spoken.

It was O'Hare in Chicago, where I got "punched in the face."

I had a long distance to cover between my arrival and departure gates – and I was rushing to make it. In a simple twist of fate, it was a wet tile floor in a men's room where a lifetime of good luck ran out. And now I get to see that yellow and black sign and the warning I ignored in my recurring nightmare.

The real lesson, my big take-away from all this is a pretty simple one; sometimes really bad things happen to people who don't seem to deserve it. And when bad luck came my way, it was very tempting to ask, "Why me?"

But the better question was, "Why not me?"

It is a lesson I learned the hard way: No one has any special deal with gods of good fortune.

17

EASY PICKINGS

Mark Mitchell checked his phone again. Their flight was still on schedule and time was running out. He peeked into the foyer of the Women's restroom hoping his girlfriend would appear. They were cutting it close, too close for comfort.

In the six minutes since Monica entered, a few others young women straggled in, yet none had come out. He shot her a quick text that went unanswered. It was now or never. "Monica! Are you ok? Come-on. We have to get moving or we're gonna miss our flight." Another unanswered try. The other guys left waiting scrolled on their phones oblivious to what would soon become their plight as well.

Mark Mitchell found the Women's Room empty. *No way she could have slipped past me*, he thought as he ducked out hoping no one would notice. Not even the guys still scrolling away.

That's odd, he thought as he couldn't help but notice several young women gathered around the Men's Room entrance, completely captivated by their algorithms.

"Damn, we're never gonna make our flight now," Mark muttered to himself as he entered the empty Men's Room.

Just over six minutes earlier, Monica looked into the full-length mirror, taken aback by what looked like her reflection. Her features were recognizable, but infinitely more attractive. She was always considered cute but this version of her was beyond beautiful; downright sexy and alluring.

"Hello Monica, can we interest you in a complete a physical makeover via advanced AI body enhancement technology? And a chance to be a body influencer too? Why not be the fairest of them all – and its free – and fast! Just walk on through and come out the new you," encouraged a soft and soothing female voice.

Mark would surely like the upgrade, she beamed to herself, *and my besties will be so jealous. Can't hurt to give it a try,* was her last earthly thought as Monica passed through the open doorway that appeared in the solid glass mirror.

"You know, it never ceases to amaze me just how easy they make it for us."

"Always is on these airport substations. It's like taking candy from a baby."

"The males of their species are even easier marks than the ladies."

"One hundred percent. They just can't control their animal desires, can they."

"Offer them a guilt-free airport quickie and they lose their minds."

"Such vain and self-centered primates."

"Gullible too. Sure makes these earthlings easy pickings."

"Almost too easy. Crushed our quota – again!"

The two intergalactic slave-traders looked at each other and nodded their large oblong heads in agreement.

"Time to board the gravy train, bro!" – and they gave each other a high-seven.

18

HELLRAZR1

Evil Incarnate

James Johnson had just finished serving a ten-year prison sentence for aggravated assault with a deadly weapon, attempted murder, and violation of a restraining order. He was, to put it mildly, a bad man – evil incarnate and a natural-born hellraiser. His penchant for hair-trigger physical violence was legendary among all those who knew him.

As a child, James spent much of his time torturing and killing animals. Frying ants with a magnifying glass, running live mice through his kitchen blender, swinging cats by the tail into the side-walk, and lighting nests filled with baby birds on fire all brought a smile to his face. He was a disturbed, disruptive, intimidating, and incorrigible student who struck fear into every classroom he entered. He embarked on a life of violent criminal behavior when he dropped out of the 11th grade, quickly building an imposing rap sheet. James was an angry and abusive boyfriend to every young woman that was attracted to his bad-boy personality, and he proudly became a poster boy for sociopaths, sadists, and psychopaths everywhere.

They say you can't judge a book by its cover, but that didn't apply to James Johnson. As dangerous, violent, and unrepentant criminals go, he looked every bit the part, right down to his neck tattoo:

𝔅orn to 𝔑aᴣe 𝔥ell

The misspelling was unintentional but proved to be more than a little ironic.

God help the stranger who happened to look at him wrong. Not even his mother could find any redeeming qualities in her own son. His fellow inmates all breathed a sigh of relief on the day he was released. The warden and correction officers prayed that he was a changed man, but knew deep down that he was evil to the core – and nowhere near rehabilitated.

When the gates of the state penitentiary closed behind him his thoughts turned to acquiring a ride. Next up would be a 9 mm Sig Sauer – his weapon of choice for acquiring some easy cash. Then a stash of Bolivian Marching Powder as he loved the way it enhanced his violent nature. All that and the right girlfriend and a place to crash. But first he had to get himself a set of wheels. Experience reminded him that the right time was always the nighttime.

Even after ten years behind bars, stealing a car was no real challenge for James. He could not believe his good luck when he found a '25 Cadillac Escalade sitting unattended, with the engine running. Cherry red and fully loaded with blacked-out windows. It seemed almost too good to be true. "Hell yeah, baby!" he exclaimed when he saw the vanity plates:

No Ordinary Highway

His first surprise was the autonomous, self-driving feature that immediately took over at the click of his seatbelt. His attempts to take control were futile as the Cadillac clearly had a mind of its own. He couldn't steer, brake, or even unlock the doors. The Escalade efficiently navigated the city streets quickly finding its way onto a highway entrance ramp. On the freeway, James was struck by the lack of signage – only standard speed limit signs, except there was nothing ordinary about them.

There was no parallel highway that went in the other direction and not a single exit or entrance ramp or even a rest stop in sight. It was a pitch-black night with no lights, no buildings, or vehicles. Just the cherry red glow of the dashboard instruments and high beams that illuminated a roadway that was descended into the darkness. The SUV continued to accelerate on its downhill ride. The trees and grass faded into a landscape of rock and rubble. The speedometer passed 180 and the exterior air temperature was approaching the boiling point of water.

James' sociopathic and reckless, "devil-may-care" nature started to crack, ever so slightly. As he soon as he realized that this was no ordinary highway.

A faint cherry red glow appeared on the horizon, giving him hope that the dawn of a new day would help him to get a grip on his situation. The outside air temp had reached 275 °F which matched the Escalade's speed. He was sweating bullets as the AC struggled to keep up and the engine temperature gauge was red lined.

The highway suddenly pitched downward in what felt like a near vertical descent. That cherry red glow grew brighter and brighter in the surrounding darkness, but the Sun was nowhere to be seen. The Escalade shuddered and shook as the speedometer topped out at 333 just as the road leveled off abruptly. His new set of wheels rapidly decelerated and to James' great relief, a highway sign finally appeared in his vehicle's headlights.

The SUV followed the arrow and merged smoothly onto an exit ramp. A long and winding road led to a gravel parking lot where a lonely neon sign blinked in the darkness:

WELCOME MORTAL SINNERS

After coming to a stop, the driver-side window lowered automatically and a blast of intense heat struck James Johnson smack dab in a face that now looked more scared than scary.

Welcome Home Jimmy!

The valet parking attendant emerged from the darkness dressed in a cherry red ensemble that matched his crimson-colored skin. He sported a neck tattoo that was eerily similar to that of his new guest:

Born to Run Hell

"Greetings Johnson, pleased to meet you. I have a little ditty to welcome you to your new home." The attendant then burst into song, channeling Jagger at his best. He gyrated to the iconic samba rhythm that he banged out on the hood of the Escalade while taunting the driver with the song's refrain. At first there was a sense of confusion and unease. Then, a realization that filled him with unimaginable terror. So much so that James Johnson was unable to suppress the spray of projectile vomit that splattered into the SUV's windshield.

The singing stopped as suddenly as it started, and the parking attendant howled like a wolf..

Johnson screamed in vain.

"Shhhhh . . . just playing with you boy, that song's been stuck in my head since 1969," he squealed in a high-pitched voice, obviously excited to be meeting his newest arrival. "Oh, and FYI, that bit about courtesy and sympathy Jay-Jay – just not a thing down here."

"Speaking of down here, I bet that was one sweeeeet ride down old Route Six-Sixty-Six. Supercharged 6.2-liter V-8 pushin' 700 horses. Woo-hoo! My favorite flavor too. By the by, I didn't mean to make you toss your cookies there Jim. Don't be too embarrassed, my friend, you're not the first to feel me that way. And don't sweat the mess either, I have a few excellent detailers down here that owe me."

In an eyeblink he appeared at the open window and whispered into a still trembling left ear, "Shhhh, shhh, easy now, relax. I just want you to know that your stay here was well earned. Not many qualify for my valet service Jim – you made it an easy call." One good puff of breath was all it took. James Johnson recoiled in pain reaching for an ear that had burst into flame. "Just warming up Jimmy," laughed the valet, "The best is yet to come."

The parking attendant pulled back, beaming, "Chin up son, you did me proud up top! So do me a solid and give me five for a job well done!" He screeched wildly again, raising his red right hand. "Woo-hoo! Come on boy, don't be shy."

This very bad man, this natural born hellraiser just stared vacantly into the abyss. And then, like clockwork, his excretory system completely gave way.

"Ewwwww. Does little Jimmy need a diaper change?" teased the valet. Tears welled up in those vacant eyes and his shoulders heaved with every uncontrollable sob. "Ooopsies! My bad Jimbo, just tryin' to mess with you. Hey, no worries my friend; seriously; that's why they call them accidents."

Without warning, the parking attendant's playful demeanor suddenly turned menacing. A small spiky protrusion appeared above each of his temples, growing longer as he quietly seethed. "Well, so much for all the fun and games," he hissed, "it's time to get down to brass tacks. Now step out of the vehicle Johnson and follow me, your bed of hot coals is ready for you – and so is eternity."

His Just Desserts

Insufferable heat blistered his skin as they wended their way through a rocky labyrinth. The air was filled with the sounds and smells of human agony. They passed countless open chamber rooms, some of which held history's most infamous evildoers and psychopaths. There were serial killers, mobsters, drug lords, mass shooters, terrorists, and the most ruthless dictators, despots, and tyrants the world has ever known. Most were still recognizable despite the countless years spent paying for their heinous acts against humanity. They writhed and thrashed and moaned like dying animals. Foolishly some cried out, begging for a merciful death they didn't deserve.

Inside his crowded chamber room, only one pit of burning embers was unoccupied, and it beckoned onerously with a shimmering, cherry red glow.

"I reserved this spot just for you Jay-Jay. It's one of our select, maximum Btu facilities, right where you belong." The parking attendant proudly pointed out some of his most notorious chamber mates; well-known names that would send shivers down the spine of anyone familiar with their unspeakable acts of evil.

With his shackles secured, the valet half-whispered a cruel reminder into what remained of James Johnson's left ear: "Hell – *Yeah baby!*"

19

FLIGHT 777

Larry Hart was true to his name as he was one of the most kind, gentle, friendly, and truly good-hearted people you could ever meet. And it was never for show, not even a hint of insincerity. No one ever accused him of being too sugary or phony. As his friends often said, he was one of the truly good guys – a real salt of the earth.

Larry and his wife Cathleen raised four children in a modest suburban home in northern New Jersey, and were blessed with seven, now adult grandchildren. Larry was a retired elementary school teacher who spent 40 years in the same 5th grade classroom in a high-needs, inner city school district not far from his home. He spent much of his free time volunteering at the local food pantry; he delivered food to the needy through the Meals on Wheels program and he was a tutor in an adult literacy program on weekends. He was always willing to lend a hand in the neighborhood, helping out with yard work and simple home repairs. Larry never asked or expected anything in return.

Larry's affable and selfless personality never changed, even during some of the most difficult trials and tribulations of his now 77-year lifetime. Outliving his wife was hard, but his darkest hour was the loss of their youngest daughter Angela to breast cancer at age 33. But through it all he stayed steady as a rock, more positive and upbeat than anyone could expect. It was his deep religious faith and spirituality that got him through the most difficult times.

Larry had just one item on his bucket list – a vacation to the west coast of Ireland; County Kerry, the home of his grandparents – on his mother's side. His dream was to sit at the oceanside enjoying the sea breeze while sipping a hot cup of tea – at peace with the world and his life.

After all the good he'd done for others, a group of friends and neighbors pitched in to repay his many favors with a surprise birthday gift for the vacation of his dreams.

--------•--------

Larry's trip to Ireland exceeded his greatest expectations and County Kerry was more beautiful than he imagined. He drove the loop around the Iveragh Peninsula, visited the Ring of Kerry, Moll's Gap, and lunched at The Fish Box in Dingle. The time spent with relatives and new acquaintances made it an experience that he would never forget.

A minor glitch came in the form of a recurring dream that interfered with his regular pattern of restful, undisturbed sleep. It was the kind of dream in which he was consciously aware of what was occurring, in real time. In his dream, Larry enters an elevator and presses floor number 777. After a very long ride up, the doors open and he is greeted by a woman with soft and gentle features, dressed in a white flowing gown. Her almost angelic face looked more and more familiar as the nights went by. She would always say the same thing, "Not yet Larry, your seat at the table isn't ready." When elevator doors close, he wakes up – unable to fall back asleep.

On his final night in Ireland, the dream changed. Larry enters the elevator and presses floor number 777 as usual. And after a very long ride up the doors open and he is greeted by the same woman with soft and gentle features, dressed in a white flowing gown. But in this final dream he now recognizes her. She says, "Hi Daddy, that elevator sure beats a stairway, doesn't it?" And in his dream he is aware that he laughs at this line, as an instrumental cover of that old Zeppelin tune had been playing during his ride up.

Angela then says, "Your seat at the table is just about ready Daddy, you'll be right between me and Mom." And he wakes up, never having to take that elevator ride down.

———————————◆———————————

Larry got to Shannon International with time to spare and arrived early at Gate 7. He saw that his departure time for Flight 777 was on schedule: 7:07 pm IST (GMT +1). His boarding pass showed that he was in Group 7. He then heard an unusual announcement, "It is now time for Group 7 passenger Larry Hart to board Flight 777. Please proceed through the white lane Mr. Hart. Will all other passengers in groups 1 through 6 please remain seated until your group is called."

As Larry approached the gate agent, he noticed that she was a dead-ringer for his wife Cathleen when he first met her 57 years ago. She checked his boarding pass and gave him a friendly wink as he entered the empty flight bridge.

When Larry boarded the plane, he noticed that it was packed with a diverse group of passengers from every corner of the world. Most of them elderly, maybe one out of five in middle age, a few young men dressed in military fatigues, just a handful of teenagers, and fewer children. He even spotted a mother holding her newborn baby. Angela greeted him at the door looking like she stepped out of his dream. She smiled and said, "Glad you could make it Daddy, I think you'll find that this plane sure beats that elevator. You're our last pick-up. Remember what you always used to tell me, "Make every destination the journey. Well Daddy, I get it now."

In an eyeblink Cathleen appears in Angela's place and greets her husband, "Your seat at the table is finally ready Lars, I'm so happy that you're joining us." She gives him a hug and gentle kiss on the cheek, and in another eye blink, Cathleen is gone. Larry takes the only open seat, buckles in, hears the engines fire, and watches the terminal slowly move away as their plane taxis along the tarmac, before gliding effortlessly toward the runway.

If anyone at Shannon International happened to be paying attention that day they would have seen Flight 777 accelerate quickly to take off, just a pure white blur of high-speed, supersonic motion. They then would have watched it climb at an unusually steep angle; and when Flight 777 pierced the lumpy, gray layer of nimbostratus rain clouds they would have been nearly blinded by the beam of bright white light that flashed through the opening. And they would have marveled at how quickly that hole repaired itself as soon as the plane cleared the cloud deck.

But, not surprisingly, everyone at Shannon International that day was either too busy with things or too distracted by their phones – too isolated in their cyber-cocoons to notice. They all missed out on this most heavenly of unscheduled airline departures. But they weren't the only ones. The team of air traffic controllers gazed passively at their empty radar screens as Flight 777 did not register as one of those familiar electronic blips they were trained to focus on.

Meanwhile, passengers back at Gate 7 boarded their slightly delayed flight, oblivious to the fate of Larry Hart and his one-way trip to eternity. Truth be told, we all have a "Flight 777" in our futures. And though it arrives in many different forms for the many different folks who wait unwittingly – it always gets there.

20

HALLOWEEN TREAT

The giant human skeleton with flashing red eyes and swiveling head towered over a big dog skeleton, fangs agape, in full attack mode. Next to them stood the massive bones of the Grim Reaper, brandishing his scythe in a menacing pose. Together, they valiantly guarded William Leakey's modest suburban home. From their boney lips to God's ears, his skeletons had sworn to keep him safe. And given the dangers he faced, he needed all the help he could get. As Bill liked to tell himself, just because he wasn't paranoid, it didn't mean that others weren't out to get him. The problem was, he had that backwards.

His lawn was not an uncommon sight in a country seemingly obsessed with spending big bucks to celebrate Halloween. Bill Leakey spared no expense as his collection of skeletons were joined by a dozen intricately carved jack-o-lanterns, a squadron of flying ghosts, a pair of witches actively stirring bubbling cauldrons, endless strings of orange and purple lights, and his newest addition, a tombstone with what looked like a human hand poking through the nearby grass.

Bill answered the 3 am phone call with a gravely, "Hello." The voice on the other end was agitated and angry. He recognized it immediately. It was his nosey next-door neighbor, the old widower Martha Simmons with another complaint. This time, it was one he had fully expected.

"Why on God's green earth William Leakey did you move your big old grim reaper skeleton to MY front yard. Damn thing peering into MY bedroom window! Green eyes glowing in the dark, swear it was smilin' at me too. If that's your idea of a practical joke, it aint mine. Wind had that thing tappin' on my window until I couldn't take it no more. Kept me up all night. I want it gone first thing in morning or I'm calling the cops. And last night, caught that danged skeleton dog posed like he's peein' on my dogwood tree. By the time I got downstairs, dog's back on your lawn. Figured I had to be dreamin', now I'm all sorts a confused."

"Well, it wasn't me, Martha. Musta been neighborhood kids pulling a prank. No worries, I'll get it moved back first thing in the morning," he reassured her, knowing full well he wouldn't have to.

"And another thing, I don't want to see all them skeletons and junk on your lawn past Thanksgiving. Just aint right Bill. I've had enough. Neighbors all agree. Town Hall's gonna' hear from me too if you don't clean up that front yard pronto."

"Threatening to call the cops on me – again!" he seethed to himself. "Tellin me how to keep my lawn. Been putting up with her garbage ever since old man Simmons passed." Of all the people he knew who were out to get him, Martha Simmons was at the top of his list. Bill Leakey had been pushed past his limit long before that phone call, and he'd been waiting all year to send her a Halloween treat.

It was a chilly Halloween morning and Bill stood on his front steps and smiled to himself as he nodded his approval. His Grim Reaper skeleton was right back where it belonged, just as he expected. So, he walked over to Martha's, rang her bell happy to be bearing news that would surely shut her old, wrinkled trap. When she opened the door, he gave her a thumbs up as he pointed at the skeleton still holding its scythe. Martha Simmons looked tired and annoyed. "That's more like it; now make sure they stay put."

"Well Martha, I didn't have to move it after all. You were most likely dreaming again?"

"If that was a dream it was as real as the crack in my bedroom window Bill!"

"Probably just a bird," he tried to reassure her, knowing full well that it wasn't.

On his way home, he called back to her, "Hey Martha, you might think about calling an arborist, your dogwood don't look so good." Then, he quietly snickered to himself, "Ha, that tree is about to be the least of her worries."

It was All Saint's Day and as was his habit, Bill Leakey slept in. Watching an endless stream of cars slowly pass by his yard on Halloween night kept him up past his usual bedtime, as did the steady supply of young trick-or-treaters to his door. Coffee cup in hand, he stepped outside, looking out on his pride and joy. What he saw told him that all went well after the Halloween crowds had left. He took special notice of the boney hands of the Grim Reaper, still gripping his scythe, but with both thumbs pointing up. His hollow left eye socket then gave Bill a slow, bone crunching wink.

And he knew it wouldn't be long before one of his other nosey neighbors would be calling the cops instead of that old bitty next door. Martha Simmons' wide open upstairs window and her bedroom curtain flapping in the brisk November breeze was all it would take to alert them.

Bill instinctively surveyed his yard before he headed back inside. He noticed a tiny glint of reflected sunlight in the grass near the tomb-stone. Luckily the coast was clear, not a jogger in sight. He bent down where the plastic replica used to be and carefully removed the diamond ring from the pale and wrinkled hand that now poked through his lawn in its place. He pulled back reflexively, gasping in horror as the fingers made a weak and desperate grab. After settling himself down, William Leakey waited patiently as one by one by one the fingers stopped moving and slowly stiffened.

21

HAUPTMANN'S LADDER

When Dan Phillips' laptop froze, so did he. It was the profile of a large black and red padlock at the center of his screen that instantly sent his mind into high alert. The phrase "ransomware attack" bounced around his head like a pinball. Dan was a cyber-security specialist and so the irony of what was happening was not lost on him. But everything changed for the worse when he realized that it wasn't his data that was being held for ransom through malware encryption. It was the name of the ransomware group that sent shivers of dread through his body: Hauptmann's Ladder. Dan recognized the name and remembered the history well enough to realize that his computer just might be locked for a much more nefarious reason. He yelled up to his wife Emma to check on their daughter, who should still be asleep on this early Sunday morning. His wife's loud and anguished cry from the upstairs bedroom was followed by words too horrible to process, "She gone, Sophie's gone! I looked everywhere Dan. She's not here!"

And so, a parent's worst nightmare began to unfold in the Phillips' home.

Emma stood staring at Dan's locked screen, confused and frightened. "Dan, Hauptmann's Ladder, What's that? Please, please don't tell me it has anything to do with our girl?

"It's the ransomware group. They're new to me but I know what the name implies. And it just might…"

"Might, what?" she cried.

"Shhhhhh easy, Emma, please, do your best to settle down. Panicking will do us no good. You have to trust me. Calmly, slowly, check your phone."

Both of their phone screens were frozen too, with the same black and red padlock. Hauptmann's Ladder had locked their private accounts as well.

"But Dan, Hoffman's Ladder, what's the connection to Sophie? Please, you're scaring me ?"

"It's *Hauptmann's* Ladder. If I remember right, Bruno Hauptmann was a German immigrant who was arrested for the abduction and murder of the Lindburgh baby back in the early 1930s. Charles Junior was only two at the time and despite the Lindburghs paying a huge ransom, their baby's body was found in the woods near their home. Hauptmann was a carpenter who built a ladder that allowed him to get to the baby's upstairs bedroom, somewhere in New Jersey. Anyway, Hauptmann was found guilty of first-degree murder and sentenced to death. He was eventually executed, electric chair I believe. The wood he used to construct the ladder that he left behind was a crucial piece of evidence, as it matched the rafters in his home. Charles Lindburgh was one of the most famous celebrities in America at the time, and the publicity that the kidnapping, ransom note, murder, and 'trial of the century' generated was off the charts, even by our standards."

Emma Phillips shook uncontrollably, gasping for breath, shaking her head, "No Dan, no. Please tell me that this isn't happening." And then, thoughts from the darkest corners of her mind began to overwhelm her.

The uncertainty and dread were unbearable. Seconds felt like hours while they fixated on Dan's laptop screen. Suddenly, the image of the black and red padlock was replaced:

$$\boxed{\textbf{03}\ \text{MIN.} \quad \textbf{00}\ \text{SEC.}}$$

Any attempt to contact your authorities will prove futile as we are not of your world.
We will be in direct communication shortly. Understand that we have no intention of harming your child.
You have three minutes to compose yourselves; prepare to pay close attention as our message will not be repeated.

Together, they carefully read the message. "This must be some kind of sick joke, and if I . . ." And Dan stopped mid-sentence as they watched the countdown begin.

Three minutes later, their 8-year-old daughter Sophie appeared. She looked happy and cheerful and unharmed. "Hi Mommy, Hi Daddy" she said as if it was just another Sunday morning, waving happily to her parents. The screen quickly cut to a humanoid being; an oversized cranium, with two very prominent, bulbous black eyes, no visible ears, a single small hole where a nose would be, a lipless, narrow, slit-like mouth, and blue-green skin that shimmered with iridescence. A staccato voice that sounded as if it came from a language translation program began to address Dan and Emma.

"Mr. and Mrs. Phillips, please don't be alarmed. Sophie is safe and sound, happy, and enjoying her new home in cyberspace. I hope you didn't find my Hauptmann's Ladder reference too upsetting, but it was deemed necessary given the nature of your situation."

"I work for an inter-galactic recruiting firm that supplies a wide variety of advanced vertebrate animals to cyber-gamers everywhere in the Andromeda Galaxy. My department places children like Sophie into some of the most challenging games available. Her genetic intelligence indicators made her a perfect candidate. We are sure that you will miss her, but her stay in cyberspace is only temporary. Sophie will be returned unharmed in approximately ten Earth-years, if she so desires. The good news is, she will not age a single day since her acquisition last night. In addition, you will be allowed one 15-minute tele-communication session per Earth year. And you can breathe easy as all of your devices will soon be unlocked, with all data intact. Your annual telecommunication privilege will allow you to see that your daughter is healthy, safe, and a happy participant in her assigned game. MEGADEATH VI is extraordinarily popular with our e-sport communities – and unlike most, Sophie's role should not place her in any physical or psychological jeopardy."

"Full disclaimer Mr. and Mrs. Phillips, we do provide all participants the option of returning to their birth-planet – if they want. We make no attempt to coerce any one of our millions of acquisitions to remain in their assigned cyber-game, yet I can count on the fingers of one hand the number that have chosen to return home." The alien then held up a smooth, slender hand with only three long, blue-green fingers that shimmered with iridescence. "Have a nice day Mr. and Mrs. Phillips." After what sounded like a stifled chuckle, their screens unlocked, and the countdown for their first tele-communication session with Sophie appeared in the upper right-hand corner of their screens.

525,600 MIN.   **00** SEC.

Dan and Emma Phillips stared blankly as the seconds began to tick away . . .

22

KILLING TIME

Dorothy was Tommy Simpson's younger sister and caretaker. She broke into a cold sweat when she read the note he left her. Her hand was shaking so badly it took her three tries to dial 911.

The patrol car arrived at their house within minutes.

"Officer Kennedy mam. Now what seems to . ."

"You have to help me," Dorothy interrupted. "I think my brother is going to kill our mother. He's very sick and . . . and he can be dangerous. Please. I don't know what to do."

"Slow down," said the officer. "Now what makes you think . . did he threaten your mother?"

"Yes, he wrote a note. My brother's psychotic. A diagnosed schizophrenic. Bipolar too, but wicked smart. Tommy insists he's a serial killer. But it gets crazier. Claims he's a time traveler. He hears voices that tell him who, where, how, and when. Told me he's the reason there are so many unsolved cases. Swears he has proof. Personal stuff; calls them souvenirs."

"Let me get this right, your brother believes that he travels into the past and commits serial murders?"

"He says he remembers all their names, all the details. Prostitutes, college girls, gay men, couples, even young children. He knows the names the newspapers gave him. Colorful names, but kinda creepy if you ask me."

Ma'am, can you recall any of those names? What the press called him."

I remember the Axe Man. Only cause Tommy kept one under his bed. Oh, and the Zo . . . Zodeee . . ."

"The Zodiac Killer?"

"Yeah, I think that's it. And the really famous one. Jack the, Jack the . . . Ripper."

"Well, your brother may be crazy, but he knows a bit of criminal history too."

"Told you he's smart, sly like a fox really."

"Now Ms. Simpson, can I see the note?

"Yes of course, here it is." She held it out with a hand still trembling.

Dearest Dorothy

By now you know I despise my very existence. I wish I was never born. I can't stop killing and I blame it all on her. By the time you read this I'll be well on my way. I'm going to erase my evil deeds from the fabric of time. Expunge them like they never happened. I'm going back before that bitch birthed me into this wicked world and I'm going to put her down like a dog. No worries. I won't feel a thing. I'll just vanish into thin air like I never happened. Sorry sis, it's killing time.

Love you forever, Tommy

"I don't believe the bit about time traveling. But I am worried for my mother. Tommy hallucinates; he gets confused. And his gun is gone. Smith and Wilson 20-something."

"That's a Smith and Wesson 29 ma'am. One very powerful hand-gun. Why did you ever let your brother get anywhere near a firearm? "

"Let him? You don't get it. Please Officer Kennedy. I have a very bad feeling about this."

I'll need your mother's address and contact information. And did he take a vehicle Ms. Simpson?"

Dorothy looked out at the driveway and shook her head.

"Anything else we should know?"

Another slow and silent head shake.

"Now why don't you give your mother a call," said officer Kennedy.

Dorothy ended the call without a word. Her mother's voicemail box was full.

"Do you believe in time travel Officer Kennedy? Tommy was convinced that he could – and did. He even showed me some of his souvenirs. Locks of human hair. Panties. Figured he coulda got those anywhere. But he had newspaper clippings too. Looked like maybe they could be real."

"Seriously Ms. Simpson, time travel? We hear a lot of crazy things in this business. Excuses. Phony alibis. Even false confessions. Mostly lies. But given your brother's medical condition, I'm surprised . . "

"But what if he really could travel back in time?" she interrupted again. "My mother never told Tommy that he was adopted. She is not his real mother. Do you understand what that means? Don't you see?"

"Ms. Simpson please try to…"

At that very instant, Tommy's younger sister vanished into thin air – as if she never happened.

And Officer Kennedy and his patrol car were somewhere else that day as a 911 call from a one, Dorothy Simpson never happened either.

23

DREAMBOX3

I used to think that I didn't dream. Like many, I wondered if I did, but just couldn't remember them. It was this question that triggered my idea for a dream machine. I envisioned it as a device that somehow could record dreams with complete audio and video playback. That thought rattled around my head for years as life got in the way, but it eventually found its way back home. However, as an ad man I knew full well that completely original ideas are hard to come by, so I did the obvious. My Google search turned up three different, so-called, "dream machines."

The original 1959 Dreamachine stimulated the optic nerve with precise pulses of light that, when viewed through closed eyes, placed the user on the threshold of consciousness. This artificially produced transition between wakefulness and sleep held the potential for producing hypnagogic hallucinations, including otherworldly sights, sounds, and feelings.

A scaled-up, modernized version of the original Dreamachine was showcased at the 2022 "*Unboxed: Creativity in the UK*" touring festival. It was a large room that seated up to 20 people in a circular arrangement. Computer controlled light pulses combined with a surround-sound system took users on psychedelic acid trips – without the LSD.

In 2024, Luma Labs created an AI generated computer program that they named, The Dream Machine. It converts text or still image prompts into 5 second video clips. A far cry from the tantalizing implications of its name, if you ask me.

However, these three "dream machines" had little if anything to do with actual dreams. It took a deeper, more dangerous dive into cyberspace to find what I was looking for. Turns out, the fourth time was indeed the charm. It was my entry into the Dark Web that literally made my dream machine idea come true. It took some effort, but eventually I found what I was looking for on a darknet market site that I do not want to divulge, lest you go down the road I find myself on.

When my DreamBoX3 finally arrived it included the two different custom-fit headpieces I ordered, each with a Bluetooth connection to the control terminal and monitor. I was skeptical that the DreamBoX3 could live up to the expectations. Not just guaranteed hallucinations and dissociative experiences – but the full spectrum of dream states as well. Features included variable intensity and duration levels – and high-resolution video and audio recording and playback. These claims seemed absolutely fantastical, however, the DreamBoX3 proved to be much better than advertised. And trust me, in my line of work, that reaction is the Holy Grail.

I spent the first few weeks in the PSYCHEDELIC mode. This feature was an obvious homage to the Dreamachine origins. To play it safe, I took daily trips with mescaline and psilocybin; duration and intensity levels were short and low. I gradually moved into high intensity and long duration hallucinatory excursions with LSD and PCP. In retrospect, this was not the best idea I ever had and I strongly advise against it. Watching my trips on slow motion replay was absolutely surreal. Made the melting clocks of Dali seem ordinary.

I followed my trippy days exploring the DISSOCIATIVE mode. The variety of options proved to be quite interesting. I was glad that I kept the intensity and duration at safe levels. My favorites were *Fugue State*, *Doppelganger*, and *Out-of-Body*. I didn't care much for the *Hypnotic*, *Past Lives*, or *Sleepwalking* options and I refused to try *Amnesia* for fear it might be irreversible. I held off using the *Afterlife* option only because that little voice in my head told me to.

I saved the best mode for last. The DREAM STATE options were incredible, and I continue to spend every night – and some days – in one of them.

I decided to get the most uninspiring option out of the way first. My series of *Daydreams* were pretty ordinary flights of fancy used to overcome boredom. They reminded me of those I routinely experienced back in high school English class. After that, the other dream states were mostly extraordinary.

Lucid dreams had a clarity that made me fully aware of the ongoings, which kept me in this mode for quite some time. Lots of seriously interesting and often pleasant dreams. Knowing that you're dreaming while you are, is a pretty cool experience. Controlling when it happens was even cooler.

I struggled mightily with my *Symbolic* dreams. Interpretation was never my thing – mainly because I had my doubts. Falling, flying, being chased, losing teeth, waterfalls, doves, mirrors, doors, clocks, snakes, and all the rest? Made me think that Freud was onto something when he said, "Sometimes a cigar is just a cigar."

Who knew that real world inspiration could come in a dream? I lucked out when my creative juices just wouldn't flow, and a deadline loomed. My timely *Epiphanies* dream turned a light on and became one of my company's most successful advertising campaigns. It earned me a big enough bonus to pay for my Dream-Box3 – and a few monthly rent payments too.

I was happy to find that the *Recurring* option repeated a dream well worth revisiting. I was glad that I kept the duration short enough so it didn't become monotonous. Watching myself win the World Series with a walk-off grand slam in Yankee Stadium on a nightly loop for a few weeks was just right. Watching the replay felt even better.

I made the big mistake of risking long duration and high intensity when I opted for *Nightmares*. The playback was like watching the scariest horror movie ever. And to make it even more disturbing, I was the idiot who turned his back on the psychotic axe murderer, assuming he was dead. Not just a painfully gorey demise – but embarrassing too.

I had doubts about my terrifying *Premonitions* dream, but I decided not to take any chances. The dream was so real that I swear I could feel the stranger's shove from behind as the speeding express train approached the platform. I've taken the bus to work ever since. My commute is a bit longer and a lot less convenient, but I thought that tempting fate to save a little time just wasn't worth it. Can you blame me?

The *Visitation* dream was unsettling at first, even eerie. My parents reassured me that they had found peace and comfort; that eternal rest was much more than a phrase whispered in funeral homes – that it was real. In my dream we shared fond memories and even laughed together like old times. These reassurances gave me great hope that we shall meet again, but not just yet.

———————✦———————

That second headpiece with the 23 Bluetooth electrodes was custom fit for my old dog Zeb. I always wondered if he dreamed – his frantically paddling legs sure made it seem possible. But now I know. And I even know what he's chasing thanks to the Record and Playback features. I couldn't resist the *Shared* dream option, and this time we ran together chasing deer across the field of my country home upstate.

--------------------◆--------------------

One night, I simultaneously programmed the *Premonitions* and *Recurring* options by mistake. To make matters worse, the control terminal was pre-set to long duration and high intensity levels. I spent the next two months watching my commute to work get interrupted when a clearly deranged individual pushes me in front of an oncoming subway train. I wake up a fraction of a second before impact, in a cold sweat. Cheating fate rarely ends well, so I still take the bus to work.

--------------------◆--------------------

And now about that road I've gone down and this somewhat cautionary tale. I've been clinically addicted to dreams for several years now. Can't stop and don't want to. When I'm not dreaming, I'm watching the replays. Quite the 180, don't you think, coming from someone who swore he never dreamed? My colleagues insist my dreams are the product of whole language AI – not much different than the 5-second videos from the old Luma Labs Dream Machine. I don't for a minute believe that my dreams are fake. That would be more than ironic if you think about it. And really, would it make any difference. But down deep I know they're wrong. My friends tell me that either way, I have given up on reality – all for the sake of the imaginary and the fantastical. No big deal I say, so has almost everyone else in the 21st century.

--------------------◆--------------------

As the years passed, so did my old dog Zeb. I loved him more than anything or anyone, and I still do. Watching our shared dreams, running together has done little to quell my grief and depression. Not even my DreamBoX3 psilocybin mushroom trips help ease the sadness.

Yesterday, out of sheer desperation, I used the DISSOCIATIVE mode to finally access the *Afterlife* option. Short duration, but high intensity. I am completely convinced that what I experienced is real. I'll find out just how real tomorrow morning. I've decided that it's time for me to take the subway.

24

SUBSTITUTE DRIVER

It was a beautiful Friday morning in late May. Will Walker and his younger sister Annie stepped back as their school bus pulled up to the end of their long, red clay driveway on their quiet country road. The lights flashed and the Stop sign unfolded. There wasn't a single vehicle in sight to heed the warning. When the door of their school bus opened, Will and Annie froze.

"Come on in kiddies and find your seats," said the clown sitting behind the wheel.

Will spoke up, "You're not Mrs. Sanchez. Where is she?"

"She couldn't make it today. I'm the substitute driver."

"You're a clown. We're not supposed to get in unless Mrs. Sanchez is driving," said Annie.

"You have something against clowns, little girl? "

She looked down and slowly shook her head.

"You know you should always look a clown in the eyes when answering. Now try again Annie – and use your words."

"No, I like clowns."

"Hey, take it easy on her, she's only eight," said her brother.

"Take it easy? Really Willie? I'll take it easy when I'm good and ready," barked the clown.

"My name's Will, not Willie. What's your name?"

"You're pretty spunky for a 7th grader, kid. I have no time for difficult children. But since you asked, my name is Carnage. Carnage the Clown."

"Carnage? That's a funny name for a clown," said Will.

"Funny? Now why would you want to insult me, Willie? Didn't your mother ever teach you to never make fun of clowns?"

"I told you it's Will."

"On your knee Mr. Walker. I want an apology. Now! And make it a good one." The clown grinned, showing two rows of crooked yellow teeth. Saliva foamed at the corners of his open mouth.

Will recoiled at the sight and bent his knee to the ground. "I'm sorry, I'll never do that again."

"That? That? Best word you got Willie? Last chance for a proper apology, or else."

"I'm sorry Carnage, I'll never make fun of your name again, I promise," Will said, hoping to calm him down.

"That's more like it. You can call me Carny for short, if that helps. Now get up and climb on in. It's my last stop and I'm running late."

Will hugged his little sister, as they stood frozen in fear.

"Get in *NOW* or I'm gonna take it out on your buddies; I have no time for difficult kids."

"Get in Will," yelled his best friend Zeke, "He's not kiddin'."

"Run!" yelled Luke, a sixth grader, from the back of the bus, "he's just bluffing."

Carny walked down the aisle with a roll of duct tape in his white-gloved hand. "Bluffing? Didn't your mother ever teach you that clowns don't bluff."

When he finished with Luke, the clown seethed, "Who's next? Which one of you kiddies wants the treatment, and I won't be usin' tape this time?"

The bus full of children all shook their heads in unison. Most were visibly shaken. A few accidentally let go of their balloons. Personalized helium balloons. Each with a photograph of their face with their name and grade printed on the mylar.

"I told you muppets to hang on tight to your balloons. In your left hand, unless – like I said. Now!" he bellowed from the back of the bus.

Carny sat back in the driver's seat, revved the engine and glared at the Walker children. "Now let's try again. Climb on up and take your assigned seats, cell phones in the basket."

"Assigned seats?" asked Annie. "Mrs. Sanchez lets us sit with our friends, and she never holds our phones."

"Do I look like Mrs. Sanchez to you girlie? Now get in, both of you. Phones in the basket, find your balloons, and sit. Hold 'em in your left hand. Real tight."

Carnage looked at his passengers in the mirror, "Remember my rules kiddos, look straight ahead and no talkin' unless I say so. Anyone gives me a problem and you're gonna' get the treatment, and I won't be usin' tape."

As the bus slowly pulled away, Will scrunched his brow and whispered across the aisle to his best friend, "Zeke, look at the security camera. It's trashed."

Carnage the Clown stomped on the brake and stood up. "Hey, no whispering back there? I told you brats, no talking. I'll be watchin' extra careful. Try that again and that camera won't be the only thing I trash."

———————◆———————

It was clear to every kid on the bus that they were not headed to school. Not even Will dared to ask. After what seemed like forever, the school bus turned down a rutted, red clay road. It stopped at the edge of a clearing, lights flashing, Stop sign unfolded.

"Alright kiddies, we're here. One row at a time. single file, no talking, and bring your balloons. Don't even think about those phones. Form a line on the grass, then follow me."

Carny slowly marched them along a well-worn path. Mylar helium balloons wavered in the breeze as the line of children approached a large circus tent. White canvas stretched taught, glowed in the morning sunlight.

———————◆———————

The spectators began to file into the Big Top. They each took a few balloons from Carny on their way to the grandstand. The kids sat across from them on the edge of the circus ring. They stared at the audience, mouths agape. Some shook as tears filled their eyes.

"Welcome to the Greatest Show on Earth," boasted Carnage the Clown, "For nearly three hundred years, clowns have been entertaining children of all ages. Today is sure to be an unforgettable performance *for* the ages. As they say, what goes around comes around. Now let the show begin!"

When he tipped his top hat, the clowns in the grandstand went wild. Clapping, cheering, hooting, and howling.

"Listen up, kids. Circus rules require you to wait silently until it is your turn to perform. Disruptions will not be tolerated." And then he cracked his whip.

"Perform?" one of the children blurted.

Two angry cracks of the whip, this time. "Time to fess up. Now which one of you punks said that?"

The children sat stone cold silent.

"Bad choice kids. I'm givin' you all the treatment. One by one until someone owns up."

Luke raised his hand, sheepishly. "It was me, Carny. I'm sorry."

"Sorry? Yes, you are Luke. A sorry excuse for a young man. Second time you've been uncooperative. It would behoove you to show us some respect. Step right up – in the center ring; hands at your side. Close your eyes and don't move a muscle."

When the whip cracked this time, the children gasped. Except Luke. He let out a scream as a bloody piece of his left ear fell to the ground.

The clowns in the grandstand laughed like hyenas. "Yeah, Carny," onc shouted.

"Consider that a lesson learned Luke. Now stay right where you are. It's your turn to perform."

Carny faced the grandstand. "Well? Who's got the Miller kid?."

Krusty the Clown stood up holding 6th grader Luke Miller's balloon. "Hmmm. Let's see Luke, how about you do some juggling."

"But I don't . . ."

"Silence Luke. We need a can-do attitude here at the Greatest Show on Earth. It's the Big Top for crying out loud. Now let's see you juggle." And Carny placed four balls on the ground in front of him.

The clowns in the grandstand, booed mercilessly as Luke failed with every try to keep the balls in the air,

"Stop!" Shouted Carny, "You're a sorry excuse for a juggler too."

"What say ye clowns?" And 16 white gloved hands gave Luke the thumbs down.

"Take him to the pit," instructed Carny.

Twister and Mondo grabbed Luke by the arms and escorted him through the exit flap.

Poor little Annie Walker was next. She couldn't even stand on stilts, much less walk on them. Watching her being dragged kicking and screaming out to the pit was a gut punch for her big brother. But it made Will more determined than ever to find a way out of the mess they were in. Like all farm kids, he had a knack for figuring things out. He prayed that an idea would come through in time.

———————————•———————————

Solo acts, duos, and trios followed, as clowns called out the names of the children on their balloons. They laughed and squealed with delight as they assigned performance roles.

Balancing acts, magic tricks, unicycling, storytelling, jokes, miming, balloon animals, and more. And every one of them failed miserably. White-gloved thumbs down gestures were accompanied by a chorus of boos, jeers, and hisses – while Twister and Mondo did the dirty work.

"And then there was one!" announced Carny.

Buttons the Clown held the last balloon. "Will Walker, step on up young man! Pretty big for a 7th grader. Kinda' plucky too. Looks like you're in need of a special challenge."

Will stood in the center ring and faced the grandstand, using a blank stare to hide his intentions.

"The Greatest Show on Earth presents our final act," boomed Buttons, "Will Walker will now juggle four balls while unicycling – blindfolded!"

The clowns celebrated Will's failures with a thunderous round of bleacher stomping. His balloon rose up, joining the others trapped at the top of the circus tent. And before he knew it, Twister and Mondo had him firmly in tow.

The pit was a rectangular hole, at least 8 feet deep. It was shaped like the resting place for a gigantic coffin – and it held a bus load of terrified schoolchildren.

"What happens next?" asked Will.

Mondo grunted, "Shut up kid."

"Might as well let him know," said Twister. And he nodded to the large dump truck overflowing with dirt.

"Can't you give us a second chance?" Will pleaded, "and some time to practice?"

"No second chances at the Greatest Show on Earth little man. But we're gonna' give you pipsqueaks a little time to commiserate while we party. Enjoy your last few rays of sunshine Willie- boy."

Twister had his ankles and Mondo grabbed his wrists. The two clowns cackled with glee as they flung Will Walker into the center of the pit.

Once down in the hole, he was able to size things up. He found Zeke in the crowd and filled him in on his plan.

"Hope you're feeling lucky Will, sounds like we're gonna' need it."

"A lot more luck than you had on that tightrope, Zeke," he chuckled. "Fingers crossed. Let's roll."

The two boys put on their game faces and went to work.

Inside the circus tent, the clowns celebrated. Ice cream, cotton candy, hot dogs, and beer. Lots of ice-cold beer. They talked and laughed while they ate and drank. Some walked on stilts, others mimed, and a few did magic tricks. Blindfold in place, Buttons unicycled around the ring, keeping four balls in the air. "Willie! Willie! Willie!" they chanted.

Carny connected a colorful bunch of bent and twisted balloons. "Hey lookie here guys, gather round and take a wild guess? Winner gets to dump the dirt."

"Monkey?" guessed Bingo. "No tail. Must be an Ape!" shouted Jigsaw. "Alien? Gotta be an alien," insisted Pennywise. "Mummy!!,

mummy!!!!" yelled Jollybean. "Oooh oooh I know," said Bonkers, "It's an astronaut."

"Nice try boys," shouted Carny. "Look a little closer – it's Willie Walker!"

And their laughter drowned out the last sound they would ever hear.

Will sat behind the wheel of the dump truck with his best friend riding shotgun. "Like he said Zeke, what goes around, comes around." Then he floored it, tearing through the entrance flap and plowing into the crowd of circus clowns. Stragglers were easy targets, slowed by their big floppy clown shoes.

Bones crunched and blood flowed. Screams and moans were silenced as the dump truck finished them off one by one. And then Will let Zeke do the dumping.

The ladders they found made it easy. And one by one the kids climbed out of the pit and onto the school bus. Will proudly took his place as the new substitute driver.

On the long ride home, he swore them all to secrecy. "And don't forget, even the walls have ears, so mum's the word," he reminded everyone.

"Hey Luke, whatcha' gonna' tell your Mom about that ear?" Someone called out as he got off the bus. A half-hearted shrug was all he could offer.

Will saved the best for last as he pulled up to Zeke's house.

"You're not takin' the bus back home, are you?"

"No way. Dropin' it off at Mrs. Sanchez' house. Her usual spot. We'll walk from there."

"Then what?"

"Think I'm gonna work on my jugglin' tomorrow," he laughed. "Maybe even help my sister with her new stilts."

Annie giggled at the thought of stilt-walking around the barnyard.

Zeke stepped out of the bus and turned to face the open door. "Mum's the word," he said. Then he zipped his lips and threw away the key.

Will nodded his approval.

Zeke smiled back and flashed him a white-gloved thumbs up.

After a tip of his top hat, Will did the same as he slowly pulled away.

25

ALL RISE

The shooter emptied his last 30-round magazine into the Ark, shredding the Torah Scrolls. The blood-splattered synagogue and 23 lifeless bodies bore witness to the carnage his AR-15 had unleashed. He made sure that no one survived his cleansing, as he called it, especially not the rabbi who was the first to go. The swat team was greeted by the killer standing on the steps of the pulpit in a perverted form of surrender. His stiff right arm was raised in salute; the 88 tattooed on his palm left no doubt about his allegiance. As they cuffed him without resistance, Joesph Holden looked directly into one of their body cams and snarled, "Death to all Jews! You will not replace us. Blut und Boden!"

When the Honorable Judge Noah Adams entered the courtroom, there was an audible gasp. His appearance startled everyone inattendance. His skin was smooth and paper white; pale blue eyes were sunk deep into his sockets, and long white hair flowed down the back of his crimson robe. He was unfamiliar to all, yet there was an air about him that cast a spell of reverence. Except for the defendant who revered nothing but hatred and violence.

Against the advice of counsel, Joseph Holden had refused to go to trial.

He approached the bench as directed by Judge Adams.

"To the charge of 23 counts of murder in the first degree, all of which were biased against the victims' ethnicity and religion, how do you plead?"

"I am guilty as charged. Those Jew bastards got just what they deserved. It was a righteous extermination," he boasted. "Mr. Holden, do understand that by pleading guilty as charged, you are surrendering your right to a trial by a jury of your peers?"

He clicked his heels and raised a stiff right arm in salute, "Yavolt!" He spun around and faced the gallery, proudly displaying the **88** tattooed on his palm.

"Enough of your vile, insolence Mr. Holden. Now turn around and listen up." The Honorable Judge Noah Adams pointed a long white finger at the defendant as he spoke in a deep and ominous tone.

"I find you to be an irrevocably depraved, defiant, and hate-filled young man. A lifetime behind bars would not be punishment enough to counter the pure evil and cruelty of your actions. I take no pity on you, Mr. Holden, for the sentence I am about to issue."

After a dramatic pause the judge glared at the killer. "In light of your unrepentant admission of guilt, I am sentencing you to execution by firing squad at dawn tomorrow morning."

"I gladly trade my life in exchange for 23 dead vermin. I will die with pride in my heart – For the cause!"

"I'm not finished with you Mr. Holden. Now look into my eyes and listen carefully. I am about to pronounce an additional sentence – a sentence unlike anything you could imagine. One that will erase your murderous deeds form the fabric of time."

"Really? What're you going to do, execute me twice?" mocked Holden.

"It has been said by family members that no sentence can bring back their loved ones. However, in my courtroom that simply is not the case. I hereby decree your heinous, hate-filled acts to be undone. I bequeath full Restoration to all 23 victims of your violent and murderous attack."

Judge Adams looked skyward and lifted his arms to the heavens. "ALL RISE!"

Holden laughed, "What kind of fool do you take me for. Your words cannot bring that pack of sewer rats back to life."

Judge Adams stood to watch the procession.

And one by one, each of Joseph Holden's 23 victims walked through the courtroom doors.

The reaction from the packed courtroom was stunned silence. Family members were overwhelmed with conflicting emotions; many wept as they tried to accept the impossible.

Joseph Holden broke into a fit of rage as he strained against his handcuffs and leg shackles. His violent threats were cut short by a ball gag.

Judge Adams addressed the victims. "I am directing each one of you to form the firing squad. AR-15s, fully automatic, of course. Thirty round magazines – no blanks. Tomorrow at dawn. Your participation is mandatory in order to make your Restoration permanent. You will be absolved of your actions and will lead a guilt-free life unencumbered by the memory. Each of you must make a choice. Eye for an eye – kill, or be . . . Do you understand?"

Joel Fishman was the first victim to speak up. "Your honor, commentary teaches us that the Torah does not intend an eye-for-an eye to be taken literally. I cannot in good conscience choose vengeance over mercy."

"Do you understand what that means Mr. Fishman?" asked Judge Adams.

"I made myself perfectly clear, I am a forgiving and merciful man. I cannot and will not participate in a court sanctioned murder." "Mercy? Did he show us one shred of mercy Joel? He slaughtered each and every one of us," cried his wife. "Think of the children." "I am thinking of them. Talia, Rachel, Isaac will all have blood on their hands, Ruth. What kind of lesson will vengeance teach them?" "This is your last chance to comply Mr. Fishman," Judge Adams interrupted.

Joel Fishman, a man of irreproachable honor, shook his head, one last time. "I'm so sorry Ruth," he whispered. The judge raised his right hand as he spoke, "So be it, Mr. Fishman, your Restoration will now be revoked." A blinding, ice-cold bolt of blue-white lightning flashed from his hand directly into Joel Fishman. The chilled air buzzed with electricity.

The Honorable Noah Adams looked down from the bench at the 22 fully Restored victims who remained. He tilted his head and raised his eyebrows as if to ask, *Who's next?*

As the morning Sun crested over the eastern horizon, Joseph Holden was positioned against the back wall of the courthouse. He was strapped into a heavy, high-backed metal chair; his arms, legs, and head were held fast by leather restraints. Judge Adams did not believe in hoods or blindfolds.

"Mr. Holden, it's time to meet your executioners."

The firing squad entered the courtyard locked and loaded. They formed a line just 15 feet from their target.

When asked, the condemned killer offered his last words without a quiver in his voice., "I wish you all a Totally Joyful Day."

"Mr. Holden, I want you to take a good look at your former victims and know that they will be your last earthly sight. I find the irony to be so delicious." After a short pause, the Judge proclaimed, "Let Justice now roll down like waters!"

He gave the signal, and eighteen AR-15 assault rifles fired in unison. His body writhed and lurched in a hail of bullets. When it was over, the blood-soaked ground and Joseph Holden's shredded body bore witness to the carnage unleashed by the now permanently Restored shooters.

Judge Noah Adams always enjoyed keeping score when his sentences were carried out. *Vengeance 18, Mercy 5,* he smiled to himself, *still undefeated.*

26

MOAB

Dr. Goodwin

The renowned British historian Dr. Mary Goodwin was more than ready when she received the news. She would soon be joining an international team of carefully vetted scientists, IT engineers, and top military personnel selected to monitor and record the third-year portal transmissions. Mary's recently published New York Times best-seller *Moab* documented the past two years of portal exchanges in extraordinary detail. Beyond Mary's historical analysis, it was her interviews with lottery winners that drove her book's meteoric success. And now, in the desert of southeast Utah she was about to become a part of history-in-the-making. Living and working in the newly completed UN Containment Dome would prove to be an unexpectedly brief, but life-changing experience for every member of the team.

The Backstory

The concept of interconnected video portals was conceived by Lithuanian artist Benediktas Gylys. The Vilnius-Lublin Portal he completed in the spring of 2021 provided an unfiltered, real-time video connection between the two cities. The two large circular screens allow passers-by to wave and gesture informally as if they were just a few feet apart instead of hundreds of kilometers.

The New York City to Dublin Portalcame online in the spring of 2024 but was beset by behavioral issues. Later that year, the Philadelphia Portal was opened, switching every five minutes between the Vilnius, Lublin, and Dublin portals. This rotating connection between countries began to fulfill Benediktas Gylys' dream of creating a series of world-wide bridges between cultures.

What followed, less than two years later, was nothing that Mary Goodwin, or anyone else, could have ever dreamed of.

The Delicate Arch

The video screen towered 46 feet high and 32 feet wide and was encased by the largest free-standing natural stone arch in the world. The sudden appearance of what became known as the Moab Portal was almost impossible to make sense of. And so began a two-year period of daily anticipation followed by daily spectacles that stirred the full range of human emotions across the globe.

The Delicate Arch in Utah's Arches National Park had been one of the most celebrated geologic formations on Earth, and in just a few days it became the single greatest attraction the world has ever known. At first, the National Park Service was unable to contain the hoards that descended on this otherworldly video-conference screen. The insatiable public demand led to an international lottery system which limited in-person visits, allowing only one dozen winners per 12-hour session. Continuous live streaming allowed billions to indirectly watch the most incredible series of video images ever telecast.

The Moab Portal switched locations every hour and offered a true video-conference connection providing real-time conversations. But what made the Moab Portal just so compelling, so historically significant yet, ultimately terrifying, was that each and every day, viewers were presented with 24 different locations on the timeline of human history. The random nature of these supernatural connections added an element of suspense and surprise to daily viewing. Lottery winners were permitted to converse freely with Anachronists, as the video visitors from the past became known. Any attempt to alter history during exchanges with them was strictly prohibited.

Mary was one of the many area specialists who were assigned to supervise and support each group of lottery winners. She was also tasked with developing trust and cooperation between Anachronists and lottery winners. The accounts of her four, 12-hour shifts would become some of the most compelling chapters in *Moab*.

The Good . . .

Over the course of the first year, humans everywhere were enthralled by interactions across the ages with the complete spectrum of humanity. Language translations were in real-time; dates and locations appeared in the corners of the screen. Connections varied from the mundane and ordinary to the famous and extraordinary. The reactions from most Anachronists morphed from initial fear, disbelief, and caution – to acceptance, engagement, and even enjoyment. The conversations that ensued never failed to astound.

People from settlements, tribes, ancient civilizations, dynasties, empires – and beyond – interacted with the 21st century on a daily basis. Mary Goodwin's 48 one hour sessions were a historian's dream come true. She and her group had many enjoyable and enlightening contacts with the everyday Anachronists. Neanderthal families, Mesopotamian farmers, Egyptian merchants, Greek artisans, Apache hunters, Viking ship builders, Roman politicians, Pilgrims on Thanksgiving, and others made up a fascinating cross-section of our human ancestry.

Billions of people around the world watched with even greater anticipation when lottery winners began a long running series of sessions with many of the most famous figures in world history. Hundreds of encounters with the likes of Socrates, Cleopatra, Confucius, Newton, Buddha, Shackleton, Rosa Parks, Oppenheimer, Mandella, Sitting Bull, Hannibal, Elvis, DaVinci, Catherine the Great, Homer, Gutenberg, Muhammed, Einstein, and many other influential and important Anachronists.

Hourly connections of pure wonderment, courtesy of the mystical Moab Portal . . .

Mary spent 12 hours with some of history's greats. Michelangelo in the Sistine Chapel. Washington, camped on the Delaware. Faraday in his workshop. Magellan departing from Spain. Gandhi at the Champaran agitation in Bihar. Harriet Tubman at the raid of Combahee. Darwin in the Galapagos. Lewis, Clark, and Sacagaweaon the Columbia River. Mozart at 14, on his second European tour. Her group's conversations with Jesus and the Apostles at the Last Supper became a viral YouTube video with over 120 billion views.

Her group's last hour was spent with a thankful President Lincoln. The Civil War had just ended, and Abe was in good spirits as he was preparing for a big night out at Ford's Theatre. After a memorable hour, Lincoln scrunched his brow, "Dr. Goodwin, I've thoroughly enjoyed our time together, yet a heavy heart seems to weigh upon you. Is there something that troubles you?" As Mary shook her head, the silence was shattered. "Abe. No! Don't go!" The disruptive guest was ball-gagged and hustled out by security, her arms still flailing, a warning that was met only by Lincon's puzzled look and a shrug of his lanky shoulders.

. . . The Bad, and The Ugly

The second year presented a much different view of human history. Video visits featured dark and odious scenes; exchanges so unsettling and appalling that lottery winners were often left with permanent psychological damage. Video-conferencing connections varied from the everyday underbelly of societies to the most infamous. Sordid, ghastly, violent, cruel, and evil acts against humanity were viewed throughout the ages and from nearly every corner of the globe. Anachronists often displayed threatening, intimidating, and even terrifying behaviors. It was a deeply disturbing and violent year, yet online streaming records were set by a world that simply could not look away.

The first series of 12, hour-long encounters left Mary traumatized – and nearly broken. She came face to face with the ruthless and the wicked. Lynch mobs, domestic abusers, gang members, drug cartels, serial rapists, animal abusers, child pornographers, mobsters, slave traders, mass shooters, terrorists, and torturers. Nightmares, sleep paralysis, and night terrors plagued her long after.

In her fourth and final 12-hour shift, Mary and her group encountered some of history's most infamous evildoers. Dr. Josef Mengele experimenting in Auschwitz, Dylan Roof locked and loaded at a Bible study in Charleston, Jack the Ripper in a dark and bloody London back alley, McVeigh and Nichols filling steel drums with diesel fuel and fertilizer, Charles-Henri Sampson with his guillotine hard at work, and Dahmer at the dinner table.

When the last of the sessions began, the world's greatest conqueror immediately locked eyes with Mary Goodwin. His leering stare chilled her to the bone. Genghis Khan then taunted her with explicit carnal desires. He beckoned to her, flashing his exposed weapon of choice. Then he mocked her as dry heaves shuddered through her body. The group recoiled when his larger-than-life arm plunged through the space-time continuum. Khan grabbed at her, roaring maliciously as her heaving body collapsed in terror. The chaos that ensued between lottery winners and Genghis Khan and his Mongol chieftains became epic viewing.

The "Goodwin Rule" was established to keep all visitors to the Moab Portal at a safe distance, or to prevent any attempt to physically enter the past.

The Shutdown

Control and enforcement were problematic throughout the first two Moab Portal years. Attempts to alter human history grew more frequent and arrests followed. The brave souls who desperately tried to talk Adam Lanza off his psychopathic ledge were properly exonerated by the international tribunal that oversaw portal exchanges. It all came to an end when the United Nations was forced to commandeer Arches National Park when historical transmissions began to threaten the world order with sensitive state secrets. Heavily guarded perimeter fencing kept the curious at bay. Squadrons of infrared attack drones scoured the landscape round the clock. Violators were shot on sight. An enormous lead-lined, steel and concrete Containment Dome enclosed the Moab Portal; top secret clearance was mandatory for the small international team of experts who would live and work there, including, Dr. Mary Goodwin.

We, The Unwitting

Several weeks into the third year the Moab Portal suddenly went dark for 24 hours. The team was caught off guard when the countdown timer expired and a well-dressed, clean-cut, middle-aged man appeared on the massive screen. He addressed them in English, but with oddly stilted syntax.

"Greetings, we think you enjoyed the first year of portal exchanges. It was no doubt an exhilarating look back at yourselves in history and what we had hoped for. The second year of transmissions, however, told the real tale. I will intend to make this brief and to my point. You have been part of an ambitious, inter-galactic experiment, and the results have left us rather disillusioned."

"We chose your planet for its abundant resources, superb geology, atmospheric chemistry, vast hydrology, and proper temperature regimes for a complete, three phase water cycle. We had to significantly increase your planet's axial tilt so as to enhance your climate variability to match that of other planets in our experiment. We planted the molecular seeds of life and directed the asteroid impact so as to greatly accelerate our goal of mammalian domination. Over the millennia, we tweaked their genetics so as to ensure the most advanced primate life forms would be made in our image. Look at us. Please admit the resemblance is uncanny, yet no mere coincidence. But we are nothing like the gods you made – the ones you pray to – and the ones you go to war for. Most importantly, we inspired a level of brain development that would be sure to discover complex language, religion, culture, music, art, government, industries, and what you believe to be, advanced technologies. Yes, the very same intelligent biological design that many of you scoffed at. Beyond that, we implored ourselves to not interfere, yet we did have some lapses. However, we are certain that none of the early stone structures we built had any effect on the experimental outcome I am here to discuss."

Admonishment

"We have spent well over ten thousand earth-years monitoring your response to the one variable that we manipulated in our experiment. Unfortunately, you have disproved our hypothesis. The apparent default mode of your species is not one to be proud of."

"Over the course of your relatively brief history, you have murdered, executed, maimed, tortured, raped, enslaved, and oppressed countless billions of your fellow humans. Atrocities and acts of grave depravity litter your past. You have wasted endless resources building weapons of war and mass destruction – all at an unimaginable cost. And many of you have mistreated your fellow animals, oblivious to their sentient nature."

"With all due respect," interjected Dr. Goodwin, "Your analysis of human nature excludes our best qualities. Did you not observe altruism, compassion, and love?"

"Can I ask you Dr. Goodwin, why you think such qualities supersede the preponderance of violence, cruelty, and wickedness that we have displayed? How could you ignore the look back on your history and believe that compassion has conquered greed, that love has conquered hate. As an historian, have you not documented how the alpha-males of your species who wielded great power, more often than not, chose to abuse it for personal gain."

Dr. Mary Goodwin looked away from the portal screen, unable to respond.

The Meaning Of Life

"The good news for us is that the implementation of our standard experiment termination plan is unnecessary. The reason will have been evident when viewing our next series of time transmissions – from your approaching *future*. Your human race will be saving us the effort to complete the ecological purge we require for planetary reassignment."

"By now you must have been questioning yourselves about the variable. Wondering, I think, just what we manipulated in our experiment?"

The heads of all team members nodded affirmatively – awestruck by what they were hearing.

One of the scientists finally spoke up, "What was it?"

The extra-terrestrial answered the question without emotion, "Free will. The Utopia we hypothesized that free will would produce has been lost to a darkness we did not anticipate."

"For the countless millions of earthlings who have futilely pondered the meaning of life over the millennia, well, now you can know. You are nothing more than a failed experiment."

And the screen went dark again.

Free Will Unleashed

Twenty-four hours later, the first video feed from the future appeared. Mary gasped, "My god! He was right."

"Right? Who? Who was right?"

"Oppenheimer."

"Huh?"

"We have become Death, destroyer of worlds."

The team watched in horror, as there would be no interacting with the smoldering carbon shadows that covered the sidewalks of what had been New York City – and all the other locations that followed. Their horror turned to shock, then complete numbness when their attention was suddenly redirected.

"Jesus Christ. Look. Lower left – the date stamp."

"No. It can't be."

"May god have mercy on our souls."

"We'll know soon enough," said Mary Goodwin.

27

BE CAREFUL WHAT YOU DRAW

Davenport's

I'm not a kid anymore, but my story started back when I was. It was the summer between 4th and 5th grade. I was 9 years old, going on 10. Our family was on vacation in London, England and we were on a walking tour of the city. One of our stops was Davenport's – a very old, family magic shop located in an underground arcade, and it was celebrating its 100th anniversary. I was so fascinated by the magical merchandise that the next day I begged my parents to take me back, as it was my last chance before flying home. They did agree, but, if I had a do-over I'm not entirely sure I would make that request again.

The Next Day

I spent over an hour perusing the different magic tricks, magic books, magician hats, wands, and other magical paraphernalia. As chance would have it, I spotted a small box on a shelf too high to reach. It was the size and shape of a small Crayola box, but it was plain white cardboard with black labeling that, with a bit of squinting, I could just about read: 8 MAGIC CRAYONS. In the smaller print below, in parenthesis, it stated, (Warning! Be careful what you draw). This made me all the more curious and dead set on purchasing what was apparently the last box left. They were a bit pricey, but my Dad willingly paid the 10 Euros. At the register I was assured they would be well worth the cost.

As we were walking out the door, Mr. Davenport called out to me, "Make sure you heed that warning kid. Be careful what you draw!"

No Joke

After a long flight, a late night, and a restless sleep, I awoke with only one thought in mind. To my surprise, when I opened the box, it was filled with 8 identical crayons. Each one had a white paper covering like ordinary Crayolas, with a single word printed in bold black letters: **MAGIC**

It was then that my mother poked her head into my room. When she saw my box of magic crayons, she reminded me, "Make sure you heed that warning Max. Be careful what you draw." Her notably sarcastic tone told me she had little faith in magic.

The crayons each had a fine point, but the wax was crystal clear, like the most perfectly transparent glass you've ever seen. I immediately assumed that I was duped. Colorless crayons? Seriously? *Ha! Joke's on me*, I thought.

But to my complete surprise, on paper, that crystal clear wax somehow turned into the exact colors of whatever I drew – in real time. But that magical quality was just the tip of the crayon, so to speak, because they did a whole lot more than just change color!

I Can Draw!

Back then I was one of those kids who liked to say, "I can't draw." Of course, I could draw – I just wasn't very good at it. To my absolute amazement that changed whenever I pulled a magic crayon from the box. It may sound crazy, but every time I held one it would squirm in my hand, as if it couldn't wait to draw. And to this day, I swear that each of my magic crayons literally guided my hand as if they could read my mind. It was more than a bit creepy at first, but I'm so used to it now that I barely notice.

And so, over a span of many years, my magic crayons and I created a series of incredibly realistic and detailed drawings that changed my life forever.

And I do mean forever – literally.

My First "Taste" of Magic

For the first test of my crayon's magical ability I decided on a drawing that was both simple to illustrate and tasty too. For some reason the magic crayon would not let me put it down until the drawing was complete. And when I did, it twitched ever so slightly before silently disappearing in a tiny puff of white smoke. To my utter astonishment, my absolutely exquisite and perfectly realistic drawing of a pizza and the paper it was drawn on did the same! And in its place – you guessed it – a piping hot, fresh from the oven, large, 8 slice, plain cheese pie appeared on my kitchen table. *Now that was magical*, I grinned to myself.

Before my first bite, I looked at the seven remaining magic crayons and even at that tender young age, I recognized that I had something very special and maybe even powerful in my possession. That realization made it easy to fight the urge to pick up another crayon and draw an icy cold glass of root beer to go with my pizza. And yes, the pie was as good as my drawing looked – so perfectly delicious that every time I think about it, I can still taste it.

My Backyard

Not only did I refrain from drawing that icy cold glass of root beer, but I waited a full year before my next drawing. I was 10 going on 11 and with a whole year to think about it I decided to test the complexity of a single drawing. I looked out at my expansive but barren backyard and began to draw – with the help of my crayon of course. Nearly one hour of detailed crayon work and two puffs of white smoke later, I looked out my kitchen window and my jaw (figuratively) dropped to the ground.

I remember running outside to see if it was all real – and just to make sure I gave my new backyard a full workout. I took my new 10-speed bicycle for a few spins around the block followed by a refreshing dip in my new Olympic sized, in-ground swimming pool. To top it off I climbed the ladder at the base of my enormous new oak tree and spent the afternoon relaxing in my new, super-deluxe, tricked-out treehouse.

. . . .All that, and with just one crayon!

Too Close for Comfort

I was in middle school when I pulled the third crayon from its cardboard home. My inspiration came from a must-pass science test that I wasn't quite ready for. I needed a sheet of black construction paper for this slightly devious drawing. And boy was that magic accurate: 18" of powdery snow blanketed the ground in the early morning, just like I drew it. Only one problem; the night before, during the storm, my father skidded off the road on his way home from work. It could have been much worse as he sustained a few cuts and bruises from the airbag and fractured left ankle.

I did get my snow day and a reprieve from that science test, but our family car spent two weeks in the body shop. My dad got a night in the ER and a new orthopedic walking boot.

My failure to heed the warning or to consider any unintended consequences of my drawing ahead of time made for a very close call, and a lesson learned. However, realizing that I could control the weather, left me wondering what the limits of my magic crayons might be.

He's Back

Another year or so older and I had a crazy idea that I prayed would work. So, I put crayon to paper drawing a perfect likeness of my old Newf in his prime. I even wrote his name on the ID tag that hung from his collar. Then I tried something different. I wrote a notation because I couldn't capture these qualities in a drawing: "A loyal, obedient, and immortal dog who can talk to me." At the time I thought that this might be asking too much from magic, but I just had to give it go.

I heard his friendly, "woof" before the white smoke cleared.

Bean arrived in his prime; shaggy black coat, the same old goofy smile with just a touch of drool. He is more loyal and obedient than ever. He speaks when spoken too, though everyone else just hears barks. And he has not aged a bit in all these years. At the time, I smiled to myself, and wondered if real magic might not have any limits at all.

Easy-Peasy Payday

I was a sophomore in high school when I decided to try the obvious. After all, who needs a part-time job when you have a magic crayon seemingly without limits. The detail with which I drew my next picture was indistinguishable from the original engravings. When the white smoke cleared, there sat 8 stacks of $20 bills. There were 8 bundles in each stack and 50 bills in every bundle – just like I drew it. My calculator told me it was $1,280 – but it looked like a lot more than that. Whatever. As it turned out it was more than enough to get me through high school and college without ever having to work a boring, minimum wage job.

This idea really tested my willpower, but in the end, I did manage a bit of self-control. No treasure chest overflowing with priceless jewels, no vault filled with 24K gold bullion – not even a winning Powerball lottery ticket. I thought of the warning and reasoned that being overly greedy would probably not end well for me.

Now down to my last three crayons it took me a long time before deciding what would come next.

Back In Time

Like many young boys, I fell hard for dinosaurs. Triceratops, Stegosaurus, Tyrannosaurus, Diplodocus and all the others. It was a fascination that never went away. Now, with only 3 crayons left, I owed it to myself to try to do the impossible. Glad I gave this idea some serious thought before drawing. I was careful not to endanger my college campus and I didn't want to strand any dinosaurs in the 21st century. So, I committed to what had to be a two-crayon, round-trip adventure. It took me (and the crayon) well over two hours as it was the most detailed drawing yet.

I made sure to add a label: "Late Cretaceous Period – 65 Million Years Ago."

I also tried something different. I drew myself into the picture.

After the crayon and my drawing did the usual, to my utter astonishment, I did the same. *Poof!*

Dinosaurs Galore

Who needs a time machine when you have a magic crayon was my first thought when I got there. My god is it hot, humid, smelly, and wet was my next. It was an unforgettable adventure – Jurassic Park without the park but with all the excitement – and yes, all the danger. The literal highlight of my trip was the scenic flight, courtesy of my Pterosaur tour guide. I got to see dozens of different dinosaurs – and more – as we soared far and wide above a spectacular, yet savage and foreboding prehistoric landscape. While taking it all in, my thoughts drifted to the asteroid collision that would soon alter everything I had seen. As we landed a small mammal scurried by reminding me that, thankfully, there would be some survivors.

Back on the ground, things were a lot more treacherous. After one very lucky escape from becoming a T-Rex snack item I thought twice about pushing my luck any further.

Well Max, I thought to myself, *I think it's time to get back to the future!*

Safe and Sound

My college dorm room was a quick and easy drawing away. Using my second to last crayon to get myself back safely was well worth having my dinosaur dreams come true.

As I lay there staring at the ceiling and reflecting on my series of drawings over the years, it struck me that the only real limit to magic might well be my own imagination.

With only one crayon left, I had some serious imagining to do.

YOLO

My college days were behind me and my imagination had been stretched to its limit when this somewhat risky idea popped into my head. I wondered if it just might be the work-around I'd been looking for ever since the day one of my crayons refused to draw.

I sat there with Bean at my side, the last of the 8 magic crayons squirming in my hand and a clean sheet of paper ready to give it a go. But I hesitated and put the crayon back in its box, worried that I was taking too big a chance on what could be my last drawing.

So I decided to ask Bean. His answer was more than ironic. "Go for it Old Man – as they say, you only live once."

I realized that he was right – after all I still had a head full of magical ideas – and a dog to take care of.

And Then There Was One

This drawing took some time, but my last crayon did not let me down. The shop looked just like I remembered it and I looked exactly like me. Next thing I knew, I was standing at the register, completing my credit card payment. As I was walking out the door with a bag filled with eight, small white boxes, a distinctly older looking Mr. Davenport called out to me, "Make sure you heed that warning young man. Be careful what you draw."

THE END

AUTHOR'S NOTES
WITH THEMES

THE VISITATION

I borrowed this idea from one of my favorite writer's classic TV episodes. I gave it a 21st century makeover and then added a twist at the end that I hope he would like. Older readers will have no trouble recognizing the source of my inspiration.

Deception. Betrayal.

SUMMER BLITZ

Every fisherman's worst nightmare. Hopefully anglers everywhere will be persuaded to treat their fish better than Henry did. I know I do.

Greed. Morality. Karma.

ZENO'S PARADOX

I learned about Zeno's Achilles Paradox from a professor back in my college days. Little does he know that he became the antagonist in this story. The theme is one of jock versus nerd and I thought it would be good to see the jock come out the winner against an academic blowhard.

Athlete v. Academic. Common sense v The theoretical. Madness. Fate.

REVELATIONS

A crazy amalgam of science fiction ideas that may be too much for some.

Betrayal. Power. Deception. Courage.

A HELLUVA BARGAIN!

I wrote this for screw-ups everywhere, especially us guys.

Morality. Justice. Desire.

UNBEARABLE GUILT

This was based on a true story that happened to a friend of mine. It was not quite so disastrous, but it did start with a single dryer sheet. Thanks for the inspiration, Pat.

Chaos. Downward spirals. Fate.

IT'S ME

A different kind of ghost story.

Friends. Love. The Afterlife.

ADDICTED

I was an 8th grade science teacher/unofficial cell phone addiction counsellor. I never damaged anyone's phone but my students got the point once I described my 4-step program.

Addiction. Deception. Power. Salvation.

LAST WORDS

A story of social justice gone completely mad. Hopefully no one thinks this is a good idea.

Blame v. Forgiveness. Morality. Justice. Madness.

UNMISTAKABLE SOUNDS

This story was written for every person who has lost a dog they loved as much as I loved "Shaggy."

I still can't read it without shedding a tear.

Love. Loyalty. Grief.

ALIEN FREAK SHOW

I never intended this story to be metaphorical, but if you think about it . . .

Morality. Irony.

ONE PIECE AT A TIME

I thought a little levity was called for at the halfway point. The punchline comes from a joke I remember hearing many years ago. Probably a pretty good piece of general life advice for most of us.

Greed. Ambition. Hubris. Humor.

SHOP 'TIL YOU DROP, THEN BUY 'TIL YOU DIE

This story asks (and tries to answer) the question, "Do you really need that much stuff?"

Greed. Morality. Karma.

DENALI

I wrote this before the name was changed. I decided to keep it because the majority of Alaskans prefer Denali and so do I. It is a fictional story that has countless real-life relatives.

Fate. Morality. Senselessness.

EASY PICKINGS

This is the result of an indirect challenge to flesh out an unresolved story idea. I did my best to figure out what was going on in

that airport Women's Room. The use of gender stereotypes may offend some, but it made the story work.

Irony. Artifice.

HELLRAZR1

The original inspiration came from a well-known AC/DC song. It took years for me to work out the before-and- after details of that highway ride. I also wanted to paint a picture of where pure evil belongs because it deserves a special kind of Hell.

Morality. Justice. Evil. Karma.

FLIGHT 777

After HELLRAZR1 I thought readers deserved a much more hopeful journey that the vast majority of us may take instead of James Johnson's trip down old Highway 666.

Love. Hope. The Afterlife.

KILLING TIME

This one needs a very close read. A flap of a butterfly wing sort of thing . . .

Irony. Madness. Karma.

MY SENTENCE

I went through a period where I was so grief stricken that I thought that it would never end. This led me to the idea of permanent grief and sadness as a form of corporal punishment worse than death.

Justice. Morality. Love. Grief.

HALLOWEEN TREAT

Giant lawn skeletons in late October have become ubiquitous. The idea that they moved around at night with nefarious intentions brought me here.

Evil. Madness. Revenge.

HAUPTMANN'S LADDER

The story behind Bruno Hauptman, the Lindberg baby kidnapping, and his wooden ladder is historically accurate. The rest, not so much. I tried to make the child abduction so fantastical, so unreal, that hopefully it would not upset any parents.

Dread. Uncertainty. Fear of the Unknown.

DREAMBOX3

I had this idea many years ago when my dog was running in his sleep. The first three versions of Dream Machines are real. A device similar to the DreamBoX3 is probably within reach. Time will tell.

Escape. Addiction. The Afterlife

NO TIME FOR PATIENCE

This story is a bit autobiographical. I wrote it for everyone who rushes past the roses. I'd suggest stopping every now and then to at least give them a quick sniff. Time is one of the most precious gifts we receive and not one to wish away foolishly.

Impatience. Self-control. Revenge. Karma.

SUBSTITUTE DRIVER

This story was inspired by the Brothers Grimm and the theme of heroic children. Clowns as antagonists may be a tired trope, but the ironic twist here may change your mind. You can take what you want from the ending.

Courage. Heroism. Irony.

ALL RISE

I was touched by a family member of a mass shooting victim who said in an interviews that no sentence could ever bring back their loved one. It was such a heartfelt reaction that it made me wish that she could be wrong.

Capital Punishment. Morality. Vengeance v. Mercy.

MOAB

I recently learned about video portals (they are real) – then my imagination took off. Usually, I don't write a story until I have a good idea for ending it. This one was different. It just evolved on its own. About that default mode of humans . . ? Will leave that up to you.

Evil. Free Will. Morality. Apocalyptic.

BE CAREFUL WHAT YOU DRAW

This story started as a children's book, but it ended up here. It works best when you realize that they are not really crayons. It wound up as a semi-cautionary tale on limitless desires (greed).

Free Will. Desire. Greed. Self-Control. Love. Hope.

ABOUT THE AUTHOR

Rick Bobrick spent the majority of his 39 years in public school classrooms teaching chemistry and physics to 8th graders. It was during his retirement when Rick became a successful children's book author. In collaboration with his niece/illustrator, they created a three-book series that follows the outdoor adventures of Davy Crockett and the grizzly bear. DARK MATTERS is the culmination of Rick's pivot away from children's books to short-form storytelling for adults – of all ages. His background in the sciences helped produce a collection of stories that feature a unique blend of sci-fi, horror, supernaturalism, and dark fantasy. Rick lives in the northern foothills of the Catskill Mountains where he enjoys skiing, fly fishing, gardening, poultry farming, and hanging out with Helgar, the family dog.

www.ingramcontent.com/pod-product-compliance
Lightning Source LLC
Chambersburg PA
CBHW071126100726
47908CB00008B/2497